THE OLD ORDER

KATHERINE ANNE PORTER
was born in Indian Creek, Texas, in 1894,
and has lived in Mexico and in Europe,
as well as in many parts of the United States.
Her first book of stories, *Flowering Judas,*
was published in 1930 and won her immediate recognition.
She has since published two more volumes of short fiction,
Pale Horse, Pale Rider (1939) and *The Leaning Tower* (1944),
as well as a book of personal and critical essays,
The Days Before (1953). Her latest book
is *Ship of Fools.*

Katherine Anne Porter

THE OLD ORDER

STORIES OF THE SOUTH
FROM Flowering Judas,
Pale Horse, Pale Rider AND
The Leaning Tower

A HARVEST BOOK

Harcourt, Brace & World, Inc.
New York

CONTENTS

The Old Order

The Source

ONCE a year, in early summer, after school was closed and the children were to be sent to the farm, the Grandmother began to long for the country. With an air of tenderness, as if she inquired after a favorite child, she would ask questions about the crops, wonder what kind of gardens the Negroes were making, how the animals were faring. She would remark now and then, "I begin to feel the need of a little change and relaxation, too," in a vague tone of reassurance, as if to say this did not mean that she intended for a moment really to relax her firm hold on family affairs. It was her favorite theory that change of occupation was one way, probably the best way, of resting. The three grandchildren would begin to feel the faint sure stirrings of departure in the house; her son, their father, would assume the air of careful patience which imperfectly masked his annoyance at the coming upsets and inconveniences to be endured at the farm. "Now, Harry, now, Harry!" his mother would warn him, for she was never deceived by his manner; indeed, he never meant her to be; and she would begin trying to placate him by wondering falsely if she could possibly get away, after all, with so much yet to be done where she was. She looked forward with pleasure to a breath of country air. She always imagined herself as walking at leisure in the shade of the orchards watching the peaches ripen; she spoke with longing of clipping the rosebushes, or of tying up the trellised honeysuckle with her own hands. She would pack up her summer-weight black skirts, her thin black-and-white basques, and would get out a broad-brimmed, rather battered straw shepherdess hat she had woven for herself just after the War. Trying it on, turning her head critically this way and that before the mirror, she would decide that it might do nicely for the sun and she always took it along, but never wore it. She wore instead a stiffly starched white chambray bonnet, with a round crown buttoned on a narrow brim; it sat pertly on the top of her head with a fly-away look, the long strings hanging stiffly. Underneath this headdress, her pale, tightly drawn, very old face looked out with stately calm.

In the early spring, when the Indian cling peach-tree against the wall of the town house began to bloom, she would say, "I have planted five orchards in three states, and now I see only one tree in bloom." A soft, enjoyable melancholy would come over her; she would stand quite still for a moment looking at the single tree, representing all her beloved trees still blooming, flourishing, and preparing to bring forth fruit in their separate places.

Leaving Aunt Nannie, who had been nurse to her

children, in charge of the town house, she set out on her journey.

If departure was a delightful adventure for the children, arriving at the farm was an event for Grandmother. Hinry came running to open the gate, his coal-black face burst into a grin, his voice flying before him: "Howdy-do, Miss Sophia Jane!", simply not noticing that the carry-all was spilling over with other members of the family. The horses jogged in, their bellies jolting and churning, and Grandmother, calling out greetings in her feast-day voice, alighted, surrounded by her people, with the same flurry of travel that marked her journeys by train; but now with an indefinable sense of homecoming, not to the house but to the black, rich soft land and the human beings living on it. Without removing her long veiled widow's bonnet, she would walk straight through the house, observing instantly that everything was out of order; pass out into the yards and gardens, silently glancing, making instant plans for changes; down the narrow path past the barns, with a glance into and around them as she went, a glance of firm and purposeful censure; and on past the canebrake to the left, the hayfields to the right, until she arrived at the row of Negro huts that ran along the bois d'arc hedge.

Stepping up with a pleasant greeting to all, which in no way promised exemption from the wrath to come, she went into their kitchens, glanced into their meal barrels, their ovens, their cupboard shelves, into every smallest crevice and corner, with Littie and Dicey and Hinry and Bumper and Keg following, trying to explain that things was just a little out of shape right now because they'd had so much outside work they hadn't just been able to straighten out the way they meant to; but they were going to get at it right away.

Indeed they were, as Grandmother well knew. Within an hour someone would have driven away in the buckboard with an order for such lime for whitewash, so many gallons of kerosene oil, and so much carbolic acid and insect powder. Home-made lye soap would be produced from the wash-house, and the frenzy would begin. Every mattress cover was emptied of its corn husks and boiled, every little Negro on the place was set to work picking a fresh supply of husks, every hut was thickly whitewashed, bins and cupboards were scrubbed, every chair and bedstead was varnished, every filthy quilt was brought to light, boiled in a great iron washpot and stretched in the sun; and the uproar had all the special character of any annual occasion. The Negro women were put at making a fresh supply of shirts for the men and children, cotton dresses and aprons for themselves. Whoever wished to complain now seized his opportunity. Mister Harry had clean forgot to buy shoes for Hinry, look at Hinry: Hinry had been just like that, barefooted the live-long winter. Mister Miller (a red-whiskered man who occupied a dubious situation somewhere between overseer when Mister Harry was absent, and plain hired hand when he was present) had skimped them last winter on everything you could think of—not enough corn-meal, not half enough bacon, not enough wood, not enough of anything. Littie had needed a little sugar for her cawfy and do you think Mister Miller would let her have it? No. Mister Miller had said nobody needed sugar in their cawfy. Hinry said Mister Miller didn't even take sugar in his own cawfy because he was just too stingy. Boosker, the three-year-old baby, had earache in January and Miz Carleton had come down and put lodnum in it and Boosker was acting like she was deef ever since. The black horse Mister Harry bought last fall had gone clean wild and jumped a barbed wire fence and tore his chest almost off and hadn't been any good from that time on.

All these annoyances and dozens like them had to be soothed at once, then Grandmother's attention was turned to the main house, which must be over-hauled completely. The big secretaries were opened and shabby old sets of Dickens, Scott, Thackeray, Dr. Johnson's dictionary, the volumes of Pope and Milton and Dante and Shakespeare were dusted off and closed up carefully again. Curtains came down in dingy heaps and went up again stiff and sweet-smelling; rugs were heaved forth in dusty confusion and returned flat and gay with flowers once more; the kitchen was no longer dingy and desolate but a place of heavenly order where it was tempting to linger.

Next the barns and smokehouses and the potato cellar, the gardens and every tree or vine or bush must have that restoring touch upon it. For two weeks this would go on, with the Grandmother a tireless, just and efficient slave driver of every creature on the place. The children ran wild outside, but not as they did when she was not there. The hour came in each day when they were rounded up, captured, washed, dressed properly, made to eat what was set before them without giving battle, put to bed when the time came and no nonsense . . . They loved their Grandmother; she was the only reality to them in a world that seemed otherwise without fixed authority or refuge, since their mother had died so early that only the eldest girl remembered her vaguely: just the same they felt that Grandmother was a tyrant, and they wished to be free of her; so they were always pleased when, on a certain day, as a sign that her visit was drawing to an end, she would go out to the pasture and call her old saddle horse, Fiddler.

He had been a fine, thorough-paced horse once, but he was now a weary, disheartened old hero, gray-haired on his jaw and chin, who spent his life nuzzling with pendulous lips for tender bits of grass or accepting sugar cautiously between his shaken teeth. He paid no attention to anyone but the Grandmother. Every summer when she went to his field and called him, he came doddering up with almost a gleam in his filmy eyes. The two old creatures would greet each other fondly. The Grandmother always treated her animal friends as if they were human beings temporarily metamorphosed, but not by this accident dispensed from those duties suitable to their condition. She would have Fiddler brought around under her old side-saddle——her little granddaughters rode astride and she saw no harm in it, for them—— and mount with her foot in Uncle Jimbilly's curved hand. Fiddler would remember his youth and break into a stiff-legged gallop, and off she would go with her crepe bands and her old-fashioned riding skirt flying. They always returned at a walk, the Grand-mother sitting straight as a sword, smiling, trium-phant. Dismounting at the horse-block by herself, she would stroke Fiddler on the neck before turning him over to Uncle Jimbilly, and walk away carrying her train grandly over her arm.

This yearly gallop with Fiddler was important to her; it proved her strength, her unabated energy. Any time now Fiddler might drop in his tracks, but she would not. She would say, "He's getting stiff in the knees," or "He's pretty short-winded this year," but she herself walked lightly and breathed as easily as ever, or so she chose to believe.

That same afternoon or the next day, she would take her long-promised easy stroll in the orchards with nothing to do, her grandchildren running before her and running back to her side: with nothing at all to do, her hands folded, her skirts trailing and pick-ing up twigs, turning over little stones, sweeping a faint path behind her, her white bonnet askew over one eye, an absorbed fixed smile on her lips, her eyes missing nothing. This walk would usually end with Hinry or Jimbilly being dispatched to the orchards at once to make some trifling but indispensable im-provement.

It would then come over her powerfully that she

was staying on idling when there was so much to be done at home . . . There would be a last look at everything, instructions, advices, good-bys, blessings. She would set out with that strange look of leaving forever, and arrive at the place in town with the same air of home-coming she had worn on her arrival in the country, in a gentle flurry of greeting and felicitations, as if she had been gone for half a year. At once she set to work restoring to order the place which no doubt had gone somewhat astray in her absence.

The Old Order

I<small>N</small> their later years, the Grandmother
and old Nannie used to sit together for some hours
every day over their sewing. They shared a passion
for cutting scraps of the family finery, hoarded for
fifty years, into strips and triangles, and fitting
them together again in a carefully disordered patchwork, outlining each bit of velvet or satin or taffeta
with a running briar stitch in clear lemon-colored
silk floss. They had contrived enough bed and couch
covers, table spreads, dressing table scarfs, to have
furnished forth several households. Each piece as
it was finished was lined with yellow silk, folded, and
laid away in a chest, never again to see the light of
day. The Grandmother was the great-granddaugh-
ter of Kentucky's most famous pioneer: he had, while
he was surveying Kentucky, hewed out rather competently a rolling pin for his wife. This rolling pin
was the Grandmother's irreplaceable treasure. She
covered it with an extraordinarily complicated bit of
patchwork, added golden tassels to the handles, and
hung it in a conspicuous place in her room. She was
the daughter of a notably heroic captain in the War
of 1812. She had his razors in a shagreen case and a

particularly severe-looking daguerreotype taken in his old age, with his chin in a tall stock and his black satin waistcoat smoothed over a still-handsome military chest. So she fitted a patchwork case over the shagreen and made a sort of envelope of cut velvet and violet satin, held together with briar stitching, to contain the portrait. The rest of her handiwork she put away, to the relief of her grandchildren, who had arrived at the awkward age when Grandmother's quaint old-fashioned ways caused them acute discomfort.

In the summer the women sat under the mingled trees of the side garden, which commanded a view of the east wing, the front and back porches, a good part of the front garden and a corner of the small fig grove. Their choice of this location was a part of their domestic strategy. Very little escaped them: a glance now and then would serve to keep them fairly well informed as to what was going on in the whole place. It is true they had not seen Miranda the day she pulled up the whole mint bed to give to a pleasant strange young woman who stopped and asked her for a sprig of fresh mint. They had never found out who stole the giant pomegranates growing too near the fence: they had not been in time to stop Paul from setting himself on fire while experimenting with a miniature blowtorch, but they had been on the scene to extinguish him with rugs, to pour oil on him, and lecture him. They never saw Maria climbing trees, a mania she had to indulge or pine away, for she chose tall ones on the opposite side of the house. But such casualties were so minor a part of the perpetual round of events that they did not feel defeated nor that their strategy was a failure. Summer, in many ways so desirable a season, had its drawbacks. The children were everywhere at once and the Negroes loved lying under the hackberry grove back of the barns playing seven-up, and eating watermelons. The summer house was in a small town a few miles from the farm, a compromise between the rigorously ordered house in the city and the sprawling old farmhouse which Grandmother had built with such pride and pains. It had, she often said, none of the advantages of either country or city, and all the discomforts of both. But the children loved it.

During the winters in the city, they sat in Grandmother's room, a large squarish place with a small coal grate. All the sounds of life in the household seemed to converge there, echo, retreat, and return. Grandmother and Aunt Nannie knew the whole complicated code of sounds, could interpret and comment on them by an exchange of glances, a lifted eyebrow, or a tiny pause in their talk.

They talked about the past, really—always about the past. Even the future seemed like something gone and done with when they spoke of it. It did not seem an extension of their past, but a repetition of it. They would agree that nothing remained of life as they had known it, the world was changing swiftly, but by the mysterious logic of hope they insisted that each change was probably the last; or if not, a series of changes might bring them, blessedly, back full-circle to the old ways they had known. Who knows why they loved their past? It had been bitter for them both, they had questioned the burdensome rule they lived by every day of their lives, but without rebellion and without expecting an answer. This unbroken thread of inquiry in their minds contained no doubt as to the utter rightness and justice of the basic laws of human existence, founded as they were on God's plan; but they wondered perpetually, with only a hint now and then to each other of the uneasiness of their hearts, how so much suffering and confusion could have been built up and maintained on such a foundation. The Grandmother's role was authority, she knew that; it was her duty to portion out activities, to urge or restrain where necessary, to teach morals, manners, and religion, to punish and reward her own household according to a fixed code. Her own doubts and hesitations she concealed, also, she reminded herself, as a matter of duty. Old Nannie had no ideas at all as to her place in the world. It had been assigned to her before birth, and for her daily rule she had all her life obeyed the authority nearest to her.

So they talked about God, about Heaven, about planting a new hedge of rose bushes, about the new ways of preserving fruit and vegetables, about eternity and their mutual hope that they might pass it happily together, and often a scrap of silk under their hands would start them on long trains of family reminiscences. They were always amused to notice again how the working of their memories differed in such important ways. Nannie could recall names to perfection; she could always say what the weather had been like on all important occasions, what cer-

tain ladies had worn, how handsome certain gentlemen had been, what there had been to eat and drink.
Grandmother had masses of dates in her mind, and
no memories attached to them: her memories of
events seemed detached and floating beyond time.
For example, the 26th of August, 1871, had been
some sort of red-letter day for her. She had said to
herself then that never would she forget that date;
and indeed, she remembered it well, but she no longer
had the faintest notion what had happened to stamp
it on her memory. Nannie was no help in the matter;
she had nothing to do with dates. She did not know
the year of her birth, and would never have had a
birthday to celebrate if Grandmother had not, when
she was still Miss Sophia Jane, aged ten, opened a
calendar at random, closed her eyes, and marked a
date unseen with a pen. So it turned out that Nannie's birthday thereafter fell on June 11, and the
year, Miss Sophia Jane decided, should be 1827, her
own birth-year, making Nannie just three months
younger than her mistress. Sophia Jane then made
an entry of Nannie's birth-date in the family Bible,
inserting it just below her own. "Nannie Gay," she
wrote, in stiff careful letters, "(black)," and though
there was some uproar when this was discovered, the
ink was long since sunk deeply into the paper, and
besides no one was really upset enough to have it
scratched out. There it remained, one of their pleas-
antest points of reference.

They talked about religion, and the slack way the
world was going nowadays, the decay of behavior,
and about the younger children, whom these topics

always brought at once to mind. On these subjects they were firm, critical, and unbewildered. They had received educations which furnished them an assured habit of mind about all the important appearances of life, and especially about the rearing of young. They relied with perfect acquiescence on the dogma that children were conceived in sin and brought forth in iniquity. Childhood was a long state of instruction and probation for adult life, which was in turn a long, severe, undeviating devotion to duty, the largest part of which consisted in bringing up children. The young were difficult, disobedient, and tireless in wrongdoing, apt to turn unkind and undutiful when they grew up, in spite of all one had done for them, or had tried to do: for small painful doubts rose in them now and again when they looked at their completed works. Nannie couldn't abide her new-fangled grandchildren. "Wuthless, shiftless lot, jes plain scum, Miss Sophia Jane; I cain't undahstand it aftah all the raisin' dey had."

The Grandmother defended them, and dispraised her own second generation—heartily, too, for she sincerely found grave faults in them—which Nannie defended in turn. "When they are little, they trample on your feet, and when they grow up they trample on your heart." This was about all there was to say about children in any generation, but the fascination of the theme was endless. They said it thoroughly over and over with thousands of small variations, with always an example among their own friends or family connections to prove it. They had enough material of their own. Grandmother had borne eleven children, Nannie thirteen. They boasted of it. Grand mother would say, "I am the mother of eleven children," in a faintly amazed tone, as if she hardly expected to be believed, or could even quite believe it herself. But she could still point to nine of them. Nannie had lost ten of hers. They were all buried in Kentucky. Nannie never doubted or expected anyone else to doubt she had children. Her boasting was of another order. "Thirteen of 'em," she would say, in an appalled voice, "yas, my Lawd and my Redeemah, thirteen!"

The friendship between the two old women had begun in early childhood, and was based on what seemed even to them almost mythical events. Miss Sophia Jane, a prissy, spoiled five-year-old, with tight black ringlets which were curled every day on a stick, with her stiffly pleated lawn pantalettes and tight bodice, had run to meet her returning father, who had been away buying horses and Negroes. Sitting on his arm, clasping him around the neck, she had watched the wagons filing past on the way to the barns and quarters. On the floor of the first wagon sat two blacks, male and female, holding between them a scrawny, half-naked black child, with a round nubbly head and fixed bright monkey eyes. The baby Negro had a potbelly and her arms were like sticks from wrist to shoulder. She clung with narrow, withered, black leather fingers to her parents, a hand on each.

"I want the little monkey," said Sophia Jane to her father, nuzzling his cheek and pointing. "I want that one to play with."

Behind each wagon came two horses in lead, but in the second wagon there was a small shaggy pony with a thatch of mane over his eyes, a long tail like a brush, a round, hard barrel of a body. He was standing in straw to the knees, braced firmly in a padded stall with a Negro holding his bridle. "Do you see that?" asked her father. "That's for you. High time you learned to ride."

Sophia Jane almost leaped from his arm for joy. She hardly recognized her pony or her monkey the next day, the one clipped and sleek, the other clean in new blue cotton. For a while she could not decide which she loved more, Nannie or Fiddler. But Fiddler did not wear well. She outgrew him in a year, saw him pass without regret to a small brother, though she refused to allow him to be called Fiddler any longer. That name she reserved for a long series of saddle horses. She had named the first in honor of Fiddler Gay, an old Negro who made the music for dances and parties. There was only one Nannie and she outwore Sophia Jane. During all their lives together it was not so much a question of affection between them as a simple matter of being unable to imagine getting on without each other.

Nannie remembered well being on a shallow platform out in front of a great building in a large busy place, the first town she had ever seen. Her father and mother were with her, and there was a thick crowd around them. There were several other small groups of Negroes huddled together with white men bustling them about now and then. She had never seen any of these faces before, and she never saw but one of them again. She remembered it must have been summer, because she was not shivering with cold in her cotton shift. For one thing, her bottom was still burning from a spanking someone (it might have been her mother) had given her just before they got on the platform, to remind her to keep still. Her mother and father were field hands, and had never lived in white folks' houses. A tall gentleman with a long narrow face and very high curved nose, wearing a great-collared blue coat and immensely long light-colored trousers (Nannie could close her eyes and see him again, clearly, as he looked that day) stepped up near them suddenly, while a great hubbub rose. The red-faced man standing on a stump beside them shouted and droned, waving his arms and pointing at Nannie's father and mother. Now and then the tall gentleman raised a finger, without looking at the black people on the platform. Suddenly the shouting died down, the tall gentleman walked over and said to Nannie's father and mother, "Well, Eph! Well, Steeny! Mister Jimmerson comin' to get you in a minute." He poked Nannie in the stomach with a thickly gloved forefinger. "Regular crowbait," he said to the auctioneer. "I should have had lagniappe with this one."

"A pretty worthless article right now, sir, I agree with you," said the auctioneer, "but it'll grow out of it. As for the team, you won't find a better, I swear."

"I've had an eye on 'em for years," said the tall gentleman, and walked away, motioning as he went to a fat man sitting on a wagon tongue, spitting quantities of tobacco juice. The fat man rose and came over to Nannie and her parents.

Nannie had been sold for twenty dollars: a gift, you might say, hardly sold at all. She learned that a really choice slave sometimes cost more than a thousand dollars. She lived to hear slaves brag about how much they had cost. She had not known how little she fetched on the block until her own mother taunted her with it. This was after Nannie had gone to live for good at the big house, and her mother and father were still in the fields. They lived and worked and died there. A good worming had cured Nannie's potbelly, she thrived on plentiful food and a species of kindness not so indulgent, maybe, as that given to the puppies; still it more than fulfilled her notions of good fortune.

The old women often talked about how strangely things come out in this life. The first owner of Nannie and her parents had gone, Sophia Jane's father said, hog-wild about Texas. It was a new Land of Promise, in 1832. He had sold out his farm and four slaves in Kentucky to raise the money to take a great twenty-mile stretch of land in southwest Texas. He had taken his wife and two young children and set out, and there had been no more news of him for many years. When Grandmother arrived in Texas forty years later, she found him a prosperous ranchman and district judge. Much later, her youngest son met his granddaughter, fell in love with her, and married her—all in three months. The judge, by then eighty-five years old, was uproarious and festive at the wedding. He reeked of corn liquor, swore by God every other breath, and was rearing to talk about the good old times in Kentucky. The Grandmother showed Nannie to him. "Would you recognize her?" "For God Almighty's sake!" bawled the judge. "Is that the strip of crowbait I sold to your father for twenty dollars? Twenty dollars seemed like a fortune to me in those days!"

While they were jolting home down the steep rocky road on the long journey from San Marcos to Austin, Nannie finally spoke out about her grievance. "Look lak a jedge might had better raisin'," she said, gloomily, "look lak he didn't keer how much he hurt a body's feelins."

The Grandmother, muffled down in the back seat in the corner of the old carry-all, in her worn sealskin pelisse, showing coffee-brown at the edges, her eyes closed, her hands wrung together, had been occupied once more in reconciling herself to losing a son, and, as ever, to a girl and a family of which she could not altogether approve. It was not that there was anything seriously damaging to be said against any of them; only—well, she wondered at her sons' tastes. What had each of them in turn found in the wife he had chosen? The Grandmother had always had in mind the kind of wife each of her sons needed; she had tried to bring about better marriages for them than they had made for themselves. They had merely resented her interference in what they considered strictly their personal affairs. She did not realize that she had spoiled and pampered her youngest son until he was in all probability unfit to be any kind of a husband, much less a good one. And there was something about her new daughter-in-law, a tall, handsome, firm-looking young woman, with a direct way of speaking, walking, talking, that seemed to promise that the spoiled Baby's days of clover were ended. The Grandmother was annoyed deeply at seeing how self-possessed the bride had been, how she had had her way about the wedding arrangements down to the last detail, how she glanced now and then at her new husband with calm, humorous, level eyes, as if she had already got him sized up. She had even suggested at the wedding dinner that her idea of a honeymoon would be to follow the chuck-wagon on the round-up, and help in the cattle-branding on her father's ranch. Of course she may have been joking. But she was altogether too Western, too modern, something like the "new" woman who was beginning to run wild, asking for the vote, leaving her home and going out in the world to earn her own living. . . .

The Grandmother's narrow body shuddered to the bone at the thought of women so unsexing themselves; she emerged with a start from the dark reverie of foreboding thoughts which left a bitter taste in her throat. "Never mind, Nannie. The judge just wasn't thinking. He's very fond of his good cheer."

Nannie had slept in a bed and had been playmate and work-fellow with her mistress; they fought on almost equal terms, Sophia Jane defending Nannie fiercely against any discipline but her own. When they were both seventeen years old, Miss Sophia

Jane was married off in a very gay wedding. The house was jammed to the roof and everybody present was at least fourth cousin to everybody else. There were forty carriages and more than two hundred horses to look after for two days. When the last wheel disappeared down the lane (a number of the guests lingered on for two weeks), the larders and bins were half empty and the place looked as if a troop of cavalry had been over it. A few days later Nannie was married off to a boy she had known ever since she came to the family, and they were given as a wedding present to Miss Sophia Jane.

Miss Sophia Jane and Nannie had then started their grim and terrible race of procreation, a child every sixteen months or so, with Nannie nursing both, and Sophia Jane, in dreadful discomfort, suppressing her milk with bandages and spirits of wine. When they each had produced their fourth child, Nannie almost died of puerperal fever. Sophia Jane nursed both children. She named the black baby Charlie, and her own child Stephen, and she fed them justly turn about, not favoring the white over the black, as Nannie felt obliged to do. Her husband was shocked, tried to forbid her; her mother came to see her and reasoned with her. They found her very difficult and quite stubborn. She had already begun to develop her implicit character, which was altogether just, humane, proud, and simple. She had many small vanities and weaknesses on the surface: a love of luxury and a tendency to resent criticism. This tendency was based on her feeling of superiority in judgment and sensibility to almost everyone around her. It made her very hard to manage. She had a quiet way of holding her ground which convinced her antagonist that she would really die, not just threaten to, rather than give way. She had learned now that she was badly cheated in giving her children to another woman to feed; she resolved never again to be cheated in just that way. She sat nursing her child and her foster child, with a sensual warm pleasure she had not dreamed of, translating her natural physical relief into something holy, God-sent, amends from heaven for what she had suffered in childbed. Yes, and for what she missed in the marriage bed, for there also something had failed. She said to Nannie quite calmly, "From now on, you will nurse your children and I will nurse mine," and it was so. Charlie remained her special favorite among the Negro children. "I understand now," she said to her older sister Keziah, "why the black mammies love their foster children. I love mine." So Charlie was brought up in the house as playmate for her son Stephen, and exempted from hard work all his life.

Sophia Jane had been wooed at arm's length by a mysteriously attractive young man whom she remembered well as rather a snubby little boy with curls like her own, but shorter, a frilled white blouse and kilts of the Macdonald tartan. He was her second cousin and resembled her so closely they had been mistaken for brother and sister. Their grandparents had been first cousins, and sometimes Sophia Jane saw in him, years after they were married, all the faults she had most abhorred in her elder brother:

lack of aim, failure to act at crises, a philosophic detachment from practical affairs, a tendency to set projects on foot and then leave them to perish or to be finished by someone else; and a profound conviction that everyone around him should be happy to wait upon him hand and foot. She had fought these fatal tendencies in her brother, within the bounds of wifely prudence she fought them in her husband, she was long after to fight them again in two of her sons and in several of her grandchildren. She gained no victory in any case, the selfish, careless, unloving creatures lived and ended as they had begun. But the Grandmother developed a character truly portentous under the discipline of trying to change the characters of others. Her husband shared with her the family sharpness of eye. He disliked and feared her deadly willfulness, her certainty that her ways were not only right but beyond criticism, that her feelings were important, even in the lightest matter, and must not be tampered with or treated casually. He had disappeared at the critical moment when they were growing up, had gone to college and then for travel; she forgot him for a long time, and when she saw him again forgot him as he had been once for all. She was gay and sweet and decorous, full of vanity and incredibly exalted daydreams which threatened now and again to cast her over the edge of some mysterious forbidden frenzy. She dreamed recurrently that she had lost her virginity (her virtue, she called it), her sole claim to regard, consideration, even to existence, and after frightful moral suffering which masked altogether her physical experience she would wake in a cold sweat, disordered and terrified. She had heard that her cousin Stephen was a little "wild," but that was to be expected. He was leading, no doubt, a dashing life full of manly indulgences, the sweet dark life of the knowledge of evil which caused her hair to crinkle on her scalp when she thought of it. Ah, the delicious, the free, the wonderful, the mysterious and terrible life of men! She thought about it a great deal. "Little day-dreamer," her mother or father would say to her, surprising her in a brown study, eyes moist, lips smiling vaguely over her embroidery or her book, or with hands fallen on her lap, her face turned away to a blank wall. She memorized and saved for these moments scraps of high-minded poetry, which she instantly quoted at them when they offered her a penny for her thoughts; or she broke into a melancholy little song of some kind, a song she knew they liked. She would run to the piano and tinkle the tune out with one hand, saying, "I love this part best," leaving no doubt in their minds as to what her own had been occupied with. She lived her whole youth so, without once giving herself away; not until she was in middle age, her husband dead, her property dispersed, and she found herself with a houseful of children, making a new life for them in another place, with all the responsibilities of a man but with none of the privileges, did she finally emerge into something like an honest life: and yet, she was passionately honest. She had never been anything else.

Sitting under the trees with Nannie, both of them old and their long battle with life almost finished, she said, fingering a scrap of satin, "It was not fair that Sister Keziah should have had this ivory brocade for her wedding dress, and I had only dotted swiss . . ."

"Times was harder when you got married, Missy," said Nannie. "Dat was de yeah all de crops failed."

"And they failed ever afterward, it seems to me," said Grandmother.

"Seems to me like," said Nannie, "dotted swiss was all the style when you got married."

"I never cared for it," said Grandmother.

Nannie, born in slavery, was pleased to think she would not die in it. She was wounded not so much by her state of being as by the word describing it. Emancipation was a sweet word to her. It had not changed her way of living in a single particular, but she was proud of having been able to say to her mistress, "I aim to stay wid you as long as you'll have me." Still, Emancipation had seemed to set right a wrong that stuck in her heart like a thorn. She could not understand why God, Whom she loved, had seen fit to be so hard on a whole race because they had got a certain kind of skin. She talked it over with Miss Sophia Jane. Many times. Miss Sophia Jane was always brisk and opinionated about it: "Nonsense! I tell you, God does not know whether a skin is black or white. He sees only souls. Don't be getting notions, Nannie—of course you're going to Heaven."

Nannie showed the rudiments of logic in a mind altogether untutored. She wondered, simply and without resentment, whether God, Who had been so cruel to black people on earth, might not continue His severity in the next world. Miss Sophia Jane took pleasure in reassuring her; as if she, who had been responsible for Nannie, body and soul in this life, might also be her sponsor before the judgment seat.

Miss Sophia Jane had taken upon herself all the responsibilities of her tangled world, half white, half black, mingling steadily and the confusion growing ever deeper. There were so many young men about the place, always, younger brothers-in-law, first cousins, second cousins, nephews. They came visiting and they stayed, and there was no accounting for them nor any way of controlling their quietly headstrong habits. She learned early to keep silent and give no sign of uneasiness, but whenever a child was born in the Negro quarters, pink, worm-like, she held her breath for three days, she told her eldest granddaughter, years later, to see whether the newly born would turn black after the proper interval . . . It was a strain that told on her, and ended by giving her a deeply grounded contempt for men. She could not help it, she despised men. She despised them and was ruled by them. Her husband threw away her dowry and her property in wild investments in strange territories: Louisiana, Texas; and without protest she watched him play away her substance like a gambler. She felt that she could have managed her affairs profitably. But her natural activities lay elsewhere, it was the business of a man to make all decisions and dispose of all financial matters. Yet when she got the reins in her hands, her sons could persuade her to this and that enterprise or investment; against her will and judgment she accepted their advice, and among them they managed to break up once more the stronghold she had built for the future of her family. They got from her their own start in life, came back for fresh help when they needed it, and were divided against each other. She saw it as her natural duty to provide for her household, after her husband had fought stubbornly through the War, along with every other man of military age in the connection; had been wounded, had lingered helpless, and had died of his wound long after the great fervor and excitement had faded in hopeless defeat, when to be a man wounded and ruined in the War was merely to have proved oneself, perhaps, more heroic than wise. Left so, she drew her family together and set out for Louisiana, where her husband, with her money, had bought a sugar refinery. There was going to be a fortune in sugar, he said; not in raising the raw material, but in manufacturing it. He had schemes in his head for operating cotton gins, flour mills, refineries. Had he lived . . . but he did not live, and Sophia Jane had hardly repaired the house she bought and got the orchard planted when she saw that, in her hands, the sugar refinery was going to be a failure.

She sold out at a loss, and went on to Texas, where her husband had bought cheaply, some years before, a large tract of fertile black land in an almost unsettled part of the country. She had with her nine children, the youngest about two, the eldest about seventeen years old; Nannie and her three sons, Uncle Jimbilly, and two other Negroes, all in good health, full of hope and greatly desiring to live. Her husband's ghost persisted in her, she was bitterly outraged by his death almost as if he had willfully deserted her. She mourned for him at first with dry eyes, angrily. Twenty years later, seeing after a long absence the eldest son of her favorite daughter, who had died early, she recognized the very features and look of the husband of her youth, and she wept.

During the terrible second year in Texas, two of her younger sons, Harry and Robert, suddenly ran away. They chose good weather for it, in mid-May, and they were almost seven miles from home when a neighboring farmer saw them, wondered and asked questions, and ended by persuading them into his gig, and so brought them back.

Miss Sophia Jane went through the dreary ritual of discipline she thought appropriate to the occasion. She whipped them with her riding whip. Then she made them kneel down with her while she prayed for them, asking God to help them mend their ways and not be undutiful to their mother; her duty performed, she broke down and wept with her arms around them. They had endured their punishment stoically, because it would have been disgraceful to cry when a woman hit them, and besides, she did not hit very hard; they had knelt with her in a shame-faced gloom, because religious feeling was a female mystery which embarrassed them, but when they saw her tears they burst into loud bellows of repentance. They were only nine and eleven years old. She said

in a voice of mourning, so despairing it frightened
them: "Why did you run away from me? What do
you think I brought you here for?" as if they were
grown men who could realize how terrible the situation was. All the answer they could make, as they
wept too, was that they had wanted to go back to
Louisiana to eat sugar cane. They had been thinking
about sugar cane all winter. . . . Their mother was
stunned. She had built a house large enough to shelter them all, of hand-sawed lumber dragged by ox-
cart for forty miles, she had got the fields fenced
in and the crops planted, she had, she believed, fed
and clothed her children; and now she realized they
were hungry. These two had worked like men; she
felt their growing bones through their thin flesh, and
remembered how mercilessly she had driven them, as
she had driven herself, as she had driven the Negroes
and the horses, because there was no choice in the
matter. They must labor beyond their strength or
perish. Sitting there with her arms around them, she
felt her heart break in her breast. She had thought
it was a silly phrase. It happened to her. It was not
that she was incapable of feeling afterward, for in
a way she was more emotional, more quick, but
griefs never again lasted with her so long as they
had before. This day was the beginning of her spoiling her children and being afraid of them. She said
to them after a long dazed silence, when they began
to grow restless under her arms: "We'll grow fine
ribbon cane here. The soil is perfect for it. We'll
have all the sugar we want. But we must be patient."

By the time her children began to marry, she was able to give them each a good strip of land and a little money, she was able to help them buy more land in places they preferred by selling her own, tract by tract, and she saw them all begin well, though not all of them ended so. They went about their own affairs, scattering out and seeming to lose all that sense of family unity so precious to the Grandmother. They bore with her infrequent visits and her advice and her tremendous rightness, and they were impatient of her tenderness. When Harry's wife died—she had never approved of Harry's wife, who was delicate and hopelessly inadequate at house-keeping, and who could not even bear children successfully, since she died when her third was born— the Grandmother took the children and began life again, with almost the same zest, and with more indulgence. She had just got them brought up to the point where she felt she could begin to work the faults out of them—faults inherited, she admitted fairly, from both sides of the house—when she died. It happened quite suddenly one afternoon in early October, after a day spent in helping the Mexican gardener of her third daughter-in-law to put the garden to rights. She was on a visit in far western Texas and enjoying it. The daughter-in-law was exasperated but apparently so docile, the Grand-mother, who looked upon her as a child, did not notice her little moods at all. The son had long ago learned not to oppose his mother. She wore him down with patient, just, and reasonable argument. She was careful never to venture to command him in anything. He consoled his wife by saying that everything Mother was doing could be changed back after she was gone. As this change included moving a fifty-foot adobe wall, the wife was not much consoled. The Grandmother came into the house quite flushed and exhilarated, saying how well she felt in the bracing mountain air—and dropped dead over the doorsill.

The Witness

UNCLE JIMBILLY was so old and had
spent so many years bowed over things, putting them
together and taking them apart, making them over
and making them do, he was bent almost double. His
hands were closed and stiff from gripping objects
tightly, while he worked at them, and they could
not open altogether even if a child took the thick
black fingers and tried to turn them back. He hob-
bled on a stick; his purplish skull showed through
patches in his wool, which had turned greenish gray
and looked as if the moths had got at it.

He mended harness and put half soles on the other
Negroes' shoes, he built fences and chicken coops and
barn doors; he stretched wires and put in new window panes and fixed sagging hinges and patched up
roofs; he repaired carriage tops and cranky plows.
Also he had a gift for carving miniature tombstones
out of blocks of wood; give him almost any kind of
piece of wood and he could turn out a tombstone,
shaped very like the real ones, with carving, and a
name and date on it if they were needed. They were
often needed, for some small beast or bird was always dying and having to be buried with proper

34

ceremonies: the cart draped as a hearse, a shoe-box coffin with a pall over it, a profuse floral outlay, and, of course, a tombstone. As he worked, turning the long blade of his bowie knife deftly in circles to cut a flower, whittling and smoothing the back and sides, stopping now and then to hold it at arm's length and examine it with one eye closed, Uncle Jimbilly would talk in a low, broken, abstracted murmur, as if to himself; but he was really saying something he meant one to hear. Sometimes it would be an incomprehensible ghost story; listen ever so carefully, at the end it was impossible to decide whether Uncle Jimbilly himself had seen the ghost, whether it was a real ghost at all, or only another man dressed like one; and he dwelt much on the horrors of slave times.

"Dey used to take 'em out and tie 'em down and whup 'em," he muttered, "wid gret big leather strops inch thick long as yo' ahm, wid round holes bored in 'em so's evey time dey hit 'em de hide and de meat done come off dey bones in little round chunks. And wen dey had whupped 'em wid de strop till dey backs was all raw and bloody, dey spread dry cawnshucks on dey backs and set 'em afire and pahched 'em, and den dey poured vinega all ovah 'em . . . Yassuh. And den, the ve'y nex day dey'd got to git back to work in the fiels or dey'd do the same thing right ovah agin. Yassah. Dat was it. If dey didn't git back to work dey got it all right ovah agin."

The children—three of them: a serious, prissy older girl of ten, a thoughtful sad-looking boy of eight, and a quick flighty little girl of six—sat disposed around Uncle Jimbilly and listened with faint tinglings of embarrassment. They knew, of course, that once upon a time Negroes had been slaves; but they had all been freed long ago and were now only servants. It was hard to realize that Uncle Jimbilly had been born in slavery, as the Negroes were always saying. The children thought that Uncle Jimbilly had got over his slavery very well. Since they had known him, he had never done a single thing that anyone told him to do. He did his work just as he pleased and when he pleased. If you wanted a tombstone, you had to be very careful about the way you asked for it. Nothing could have been more impersonal and faraway than his tone and manner of talking about slavery, but they wriggled a little and felt guilty. Paul would have changed the subject, but Miranda, the little quick one, wanted to know the worst. "Did they act like that to you, Uncle Jimbilly?" she asked.

"No, *mam*," said Uncle Jimbilly. "Now whut name you want on dis one? Dey nevah did. Dey done 'em dat way in the rice swamps. I always worked right here close to the house or in town with Miss Sophia. Down in the swamps . . ."

"Didn't they ever die, Uncle Jimbilly?" asked Paul.

"Cose dey died," said Uncle Jimbilly, "cose dey died—dey died," he went on, pursing his mouth gloomily, "by de thousands and tens upon thousands."

"Can you carve 'Safe in Heaven' on that, Uncle

Jimbilly?" asked Maria in her pleasant, mincing voice.

"To put over a tame jackrabbit, Missy?" asked Uncle Jimbilly indignantly. He was very religious. "A heathen like dat? No, *mam*. In de swamps dey used to stake 'em out all day and all night, and all day and all night and all day wid dey hans and feet tied so dey couldn't scretch and let de muskeeters eat 'em alive. De muskeeters 'ud bite 'em tell dey was all swole up like a balloon all over, and you could heah 'em howlin and prayin all ovah the swamp. Yassuh. Dat was it. And nary a drop of watah noh a moufful of braid . . . Yassuh, dat's it. Lawd, dey done it. Hosanna! Now take dis yere tombstone and don't bother me no more . . . or I'll . . ."

Uncle Jimbilly was apt to be suddenly annoyed and you never knew why. He was easily put out about things, but his threats were always so exorbitant that not even the most credulous child could be terrified by them. He was always going to do something quite horrible to somebody and then he was going to dispose of the remains in a revolting manner. He was going to skin somebody alive and nail the hide on the barn door, or he was just getting ready to cut off somebody's ears with a hatchet and pin them on Bongo, the crop-eared brindle dog. He was often all prepared in his mind to pull somebody's teeth and make a set of false teeth for Ole Man Ronk. . . . Ole Man Ronk was a tramp who had been living all summer in the little cabin behind the smokehouse. He got his rations along with the Negroes and sat all day mumbling his naked gums. He had skimpy black whiskers which appeared to be set in wax, and angry red eyelids. He took morphine, it was said; but what morphine might be, or how he took it, or why, no one seemed to know. . . . Nothing could have been more unpleasant than the notion that one's teeth might be given to Ole Man Ronk.

The reason why Uncle Jimbilly never did any of these things he threatened was, he said, because he never could get round to them. He always had so much other work on hand he never seemed to get caught up on it. But some day, somebody was going to get a mighty big surprise, and meanwhile everybody had better look out.

The Circus

THE long planks set on trestles rose one above the other to a monstrous height and stretched dizzyingly in a wide oval ring. They were packed with people—"lak fleas on a dog's ear," said Dicey, holding Miranda's hand firmly and looking about her with disapproval. The white billows of enormous canvas sagged overhead, held up by three poles set evenly apart down the center. The family, when seated, occupied almost a whole section on one level.

On one side of them in a long row sat Father, sister Maria, brother Paul, Grandmother; great-aunt Keziah, cousin Keziah, and second-cousin Keziah, who had just come down from Kentucky on a visit; uncle Charles Breaux, cousin Charles Breaux, and aunt Marie-Anne Breaux. On the other side sat small cousin Lucie Breaux, big cousin Paul Gay, great-aunt Sally Gay (who took snuff and was therefore a disgrace to the family); two strange, extremely handsome young men who might be cousins but who were certainly in love with cousin Miranda Gay; and cousin Miranda Gay herself, a most dashing young lady with crisp silk skirts, a half dozen of them at once, a lovely perfume and wonderful black curly hair above enormous wild gray eyes, "like a colt's," Father said. Miranda hoped to be exactly like her when she grew up. Hanging to Dicey's arm she leaned out and waved to cousin Miranda, who waved back smiling, and the strange young men waved to her also. Miranda was most fearfully excited. It was her first circus; it might also be her last because the whole family had combined to persuade Grandmother to allow her to come with them. "Very well, this once," Grandmother said, "since it's a family reunion."

This once! This once! She could not look hard enough at everything. She even peeped down between the wide crevices of the piled-up plank seats, where she was astonished to see odd-looking, roughly dressed little boys peeping up from the dust below. They were squatted in little heaps, staring up quietly. She looked squarely into the eyes of one, who returned her a look so peculiar she gazed and gazed, trying to understand it. It was a bold grinning stare without any kind of friendliness in it. He was a thin, dirty little boy with a floppy old checkerboard cap pulled over crumpled red ears and dust-colored hair. As she gazed he nudged the little boy next to him, whispered, and the second little boy caught her eye. This was too much. Miranda pulled Dicey's sleeve. "Dicey, what are those little boys doing down there?" "Down where?" asked Dicey, but she seemed to know already, for she bent over and looked through the crevice, drew her knees together and her skirts around her, and said severely: "You jus mind yo' own business and stop throwin' yo' legs around that way. Don't you pay any mind. Plenty o' monkeys right here in the show widout you studyin dat kind."

An enormous brass band seemed to explode right at Miranda's ear. She jumped, quivered, thrilled blindly and almost forgot to breathe as sound and color and smell rushed together and poured through her skin and hair and beat in her head and hands and feet and pit of her stomach. "Oh," she called out in her panic, closing her eyes and seizing Dicey's hand hard. The flaring lights burned through her lids, a roar of laughter like rage drowned out the steady raging of the drums and horns. She opened her eyes . . . A creature in a blousy white overall with ruffles at the neck and ankles, with bone-white skull and chalk-white face, with tufted eyebrows far apart in the middle of his forehead, the lids in a black sharp angle, a long scarlet mouth stretching back into sunken cheeks, turned up at the corners in a perpetual bitter grimace of pain, astonishment, not smiling, pranced along a wire stretched down the center of the ring, balancing a long thin pole with little wheels at either end. Miranda thought at first he was walking on air, or flying, and this did not surprise her; but when she saw the wire, she was terrified. High above their heads the inhuman figure pranced, spinning the little wheels. He paused, slipped, the flapping white leg waved in space; he staggered, wobbled, slipped sidewise, plunged, and caught the wire with frantic knee, hanging there upside down, the other leg waving like a feeler above his head; slipped once more, caught by one frenzied

41

heel, and swung back and forth like a scarf. . . .
The crowd roared with savage delight, shrieks of
dreadful laughter like devils in delicious torment.
. . . Miranda shrieked too, with real pain, clutching
at her stomach with her knees drawn up. . . . The
man on the wire, hanging by his foot, turned his
head like a seal from side to side and blew sneering
kisses from his cruel mouth. Then Miranda covered
her eyes and screamed, the tears pouring over her
cheeks and chin.

"Take her home," said her father, "get her out of
here at once," but the laughter was not wiped from
his face. He merely glanced at her and back to the
ring. "Take her away, Dicey," called the Grandmother, from under her half-raised crepe veil. Dicey,
rebelliously, very slowly, without taking her gaze
from the white figure swaying on the wire, rose,
seized the limp, suffering bundle, prodded and
lumped her way over knees and feet, through the
crowd, down the levels of the scaffolding, across a
space of sandy tanbark, out through a flap in the
tent. Miranda was crying steadily with an occa-
sional hiccough. A dwarf was standing in the en-
trance, wearing a little woolly beard, a pointed cap,
tight red breeches, long shoes with turned-up toes.
He carried a thin white wand. Miranda almost
touched him before she saw him, her distorted face
with its open mouth and glistening tears almost level
with his. He leaned forward and peered at her with
kind, not-human golden eyes, like a near-sighted dog:
then made a horrid grimace at her, imitating her own
face. Miranda struck at him in sheer ill temper,

screaming. Dicey drew her away quickly, but not before Miranda had seen in his face, suddenly, a look of haughty, remote displeasure, a true grown-up look. She knew it well. It chilled her with a new kind of fear: she had not believed he was really human.

"Raincheck, get your raincheck!" said a very disagreeable-looking fellow as they passed. Dicey turned toward him almost in tears herself. "Mister, caint you see I won't be able to git back? I got this young un to see to. . . . What good dat lil piece of paper goin to do *me?*" All the way home she was cross, and grumbled under her breath: little ole meany . . . little ole scare-cat . . . gret big baby . . . never go nowhere . . . never see nothin . . . come on here now, hurry up—always ruinin everything for othah folks . . . won't let anybody rest a minute, won't let anybody have any good times . . . come on here now, you wanted to go home and you're going there . . . snatching Miranda along, vicious but cautious, careful not to cross the line where Miranda could say outright: "Dicey did this or said this to me . . ." Dicey was allowed a certain freedom up to a point.

The family trooped into the house just before dark and scattered out all over it. From every room came the sound of chatter and laughter. The other children told Miranda what she had missed: wonderful little ponies with plumes and bells on their bridles, ridden by darling little monkeys in velvet jackets and peaked hats . . . trained white goats that danced . . . a baby elephant that crossed his front feet and leaned against his cage and opened his mouth to be fed, *such* a baby! . . . more clowns, funnier than the first one even . . . beautiful ladies with bright yellow hair, wearing white silk tights with red satin sashes, had performed on white trapezes; they also had hung by their toes, but how gracefully, like flying birds! Huge white horses had lolloped around and round the ring with men and women dancing on their backs! One man had swung by his teeth from the top of the tent and another had put his head in a lion's mouth. Ah, what she had not missed! Everybody had been enjoying themselves while she was missing her first big circus and spoiling the day for Dicey. Poor Dicey. Poor dear Dicey. The other children who hadn't thought of Dicey until that moment, mourned over her with sad mouths, their malicious eyes watching Miranda squirm. Dicey had been looking forward for weeks to this day! And then Miranda must get scared— "Can you *imagine* being afraid of that funny old clown?" each one asked the other, and then they smiled pityingly on Miranda. . . .

Then too, it had been a very important occasion in another way: it was the first time Grandmother had ever allowed herself to be persuaded to go to the circus. One could not gather, from her rather generalized opinions, whether there had been no circuses when she was young, or there had been and it was not proper to see them. At any rate for her usual sound reasons, Grandmother had never approved of circuses, and though she would not deny she had been amused somewhat, still there had been sights and

44

sounds in this one which she maintained were, to say the least, not particularly edifying to the young. Her son Harry, who came in while the children made an early supper, looked at their illuminated faces, all the brothers and sisters and visiting cousins, and said, "This basket of young doesn't seem to be much damaged." His mother said, "The fruits of their present are in a future so far off, neither of us may live to know whether harm has been done or not. That is the trouble," and she went on ladling out hot milk to pour over their buttered toast. Miranda was sitting silent, her underlip drooping. Her father smiled at her. "You missed it, Baby," he said softly, "and what good did that do you?"

Miranda burst again into tears: had to be taken away at last, and her supper was brought up to her. Dicey was exasperated and silent. Miranda could not eat. She tried, as if she were really remembering them, to think of the beautiful wild beings in white satin and spangles and red sashes who danced and frolicked on the trapezes; of the sweet little furry ponies and the lovely pet monkeys in their comical clothes. She fell asleep, and her invented memories gave way before her real ones, the bitter terrified face of the man in blowsy white falling to his death —ah, the cruel joke!—and the terrible grimace of the unsmiling dwarf. She screamed in her sleep and sat up crying for deliverance from her torments.

Dicey came, her cross, sleepy eyes half-closed, her big dark mouth pouted, thumping the floor with her thick bare feet. "I *swear*," she said, in a violent hoarse whisper. "What the matter with you? You need a good spankin, I *swear!* Wakin everybody up like this . . ."

Miranda was completely subjugated by her fears. She had a way of answering Dicey back. She would say, "Oh, hush up, Dicey." Or she would say, "I don't have to mind *you.* I don't have to mind anybody but my grandmother," which was provokingly true. And she would say, "You don't know what you're talking about." The day just past had changed that. Miranda sincerely did not want anybody, not even Dicey, to be cross with her. Ordinarily she did not care how cross she made the harassed adults around her. Now if Dicey must be cross, she still did not really care, if only Dicey might not turn out the lights and leave her to the fathomless terrors of the darkness where sleep could overtake her once more. She hugged Dicey with both arms, crying, "Don't, don't leave me. *Don't* be so angry! I c-c-can't b-bear it!"

Dicey lay down beside her with a long moaning sigh, which meant that she was collecting her patience and making up her mind to remember that she was a Christian and must bear her cross. "Now you go to sleep," she said, in her usual warm being-good voice. "Now you jes shut yo eyes and go to sleep. I ain't going to leave you. Dicey ain't mad at nobody . . . *no*body in the whole worl'. . . ."

The Last Leaf

OLD NANNIE sat hunched upon herself expecting her own death momentarily. The Grandmother had said to her at parting, with the easy prophecy of the aged, that this might be their last farewell on earth; they embraced and kissed each other on the cheeks, and once more promised to meet each other in heaven. Nannie was prepared to start her journey at once. The children gathered around her: "Aunt Nannie, never you mind! We love you!" She paid no attention; she did not care whether they loved her or not. Years afterward, Maria, the elder girl, thought with a pang, they had not really been so very nice to Aunt Nannie. They went on depending upon her as they always had, letting her assume more burdens and more, allowing her to work harder than she should have. The old woman grew silent, hunched over more deeply—she was thin and tall also, with a nobly modeled Negro face, worn to the bone and a thick fine sooty black, no mixed blood in Nannie—and her spine seemed suddenly to have given way. They could hear her groaning at night on her knees beside her bed, asking God to let her rest.

When a black family moved out of a little cabin across the narrow creek, the first cabin empty for years, Nannie went down to look at it. She came back and asked Mister Harry, "Whut you aim to do wid dat cabin?" Mister Harry said, "Nothing," he supposed; and Nannie asked for it. She wanted a house of her own, she said; in her whole life she never had a place of her very own. Mister Harry said, of course she could have it. But the whole family was surprised, a little wounded. "Lemme go there and pass my last days in peace, chil'ren," she said. They had the place scrubbed and whitewashed, shelves put in and the chimney cleaned, they fixed Nannie up with a good bed and a fairly good carpet and allowed her to take all sorts of odds and ends from the house. It was astonishing to discover that Nannie had always liked and hoped to own certain things, she had seemed so contented and wantless. She moved away, and as the children said afterwards to each other, it was almost funny and certainly very sweet to see how she tried not to be too happy the day she left, but they felt rather put upon, just the same.

Thereafter she sat in the serene idleness of making patchwork and braiding woolen rugs. Her grandchildren and her white family visited her, and all kinds of white persons who had never owned a soul related to Nannie, went to see her, to buy her rugs or leave little presents with her.

She had always worn black wool dresses, or black and white figured calico with starchy white aprons and a white ruffled mobcap, or a black taffety cap for

Sundays. She had been finicking precise and neat in her ways, and she still was. But she was no more the faithful old servant Nannie, a freed slave: she was an aged Bantu woman of independent means, sitting on the steps, breathing the free air. She began wearing a blue bandanna wrapped around her head, and at the age of eighty-five she took to smoking a corncob pipe. The black iris of the deep, withdrawn old eyes turned a chocolate brown and seemed to spread over the whole surface of the eyeball. As her sight failed, the eyelids crinkled and drew in, so that her face was like an eyeless mask.

The children, brought up in an out-of-date sentimental way of thinking, had always complacently believed that Nannie was a real member of the family, perfectly happy with them, and this rebuke, so quietly and firmly administered, chastened them somewhat. The lesson sank in as the years went on and Nannie continued to sit on the doorstep of her cabin. They were growing up, times were changing, the old world was sliding from under their feet, they had not yet laid hold of the new one. They missed Nannie every day. As their fortunes went down, and they had very few servants, they needed her terribly. They realized how much the old woman had done for them, simply by seeing how, almost immediately after she went, everything slackened, lost tone, went off edge. Work did not accomplish itself as it once had. They had not learned how to work for themselves, they were all lazy and incapable of sustained effort or planning. They had not been taught and they had not yet educated themselves. Now and then Nannie would come back up the hill for a visit. She worked then almost as she had before, with a kind of satisfaction in proving to them that she had been almost indispensable. They would miss her more than ever when she went away. To show their gratitude, and their hope that she would come again, they would heap upon her baskets and bales of the precious rubbish she loved, and one of her great grandsons Skid or Hasty would push them away beside her on a wheelbarrow. She would again for a moment be the amiable, dependent, like-one-of-the-family old servant: "I know my chil'ren won't let me go away empty-handed."

Uncle Jimbilly still pottered around, mending harness, currying horses, patching fences, now and then setting out a few plants or loosening the earth around shrubs in the spring. He muttered perpetually to himself, his blue mouth always moving in an endless disjointed comment on things past and present, and even to come, no doubt, though there was nothing about him that suggested any connection with even the nearest future . . . Maria had not realized until after her grandmother's death that Uncle Jimbilly and Aunt Nannie were husband and wife. . . . That marriage of convenience, in which they had been mated with truly royal policy, with an eye to the blood and family stability, had dissolved of itself between them when the reasons for its being had likewise dissolved. . . . They took no notice whatever of each other's existence, they seemed to forget they had children together (each spoke of "my children"), they had stored up no common memories that either wished to keep. Aunt Nannie moved away into her own house without even a glance or thought for Uncle Jimbilly, and he did not seem to notice that she was gone. . . . He slept in a little attic over the smoke-house, and ate in the kitchen at odd hours, and did as he pleased, lonely as a wandering spirit and almost as invisible. . . . But one day he passed by the little house and saw Aunt Nannie sitting on her steps with her pipe. He sat down awhile, groaning a little as he bent himself into angles, and sunned himself like a weary old dog. He would have stayed on from that minute, but Nannie would not have him. "Whut you doin with all this big house to yoself?" he wanted to know. " 'Tain't no more than just enough fo' me," she told him pointedly; "I don' aim to pass my las' days waitin on no man," she added, "I've served my time, I've done my do, and dat's all." So Uncle Jimbilly crept back up the hill and into his smoke-house attic, and never went near her again. . . .

On summer evenings she sat by herself long after dark, smoking to keep away the mosquitoes, until she was ready to sleep. She said she wasn't afraid of anything: never had been, never expected to be. She had long ago got in the way of thinking that night was a blessing, it brought the time when she didn't have to work any more until tomorrow. Even after she stopped working for good and all, she still looked forward with longing to the night, as if all the accumulated fatigues of her life, lying now embedded in her bones, still begged for easement. But when night came, she remembered that she didn't have to get up in the morning until she was ready. So she would sit in the luxury of having at her disposal all of God's good time there was in this world.

When Mister Harry, in the old days, had stood out against her word in some petty dispute, she could always get the better of him by slapping her slatty old chest with the flat of her long hand and crying out: "Why, Mister Harry, you, ain't you shamed to talk lak dat to me? I nuhsed you at dis bosom!"

Harry knew this was not literally true. She had nursed three of his elder brothers; but he always said at once, "All right, Mammy, all right, for God's sake!"—precisely as he said it to his own mother, exploding in his natural irascibility as if he hoped to clear the air somewhat of the smothering matriarchal tyranny to which he had been delivered by the death of his father. Still he submitted, being of that latest generation of sons who acknowledged, however reluctantly, however bitterly, their mystical never to be forgiven debt to the womb that bore them, and the breast that suckled them.

The Grave

THE Grandfather, dead for more than thirty years, had been twice disturbed in his long repose by the constancy and possessiveness of his widow. She removed his bones first to Louisiana and then to Texas as if she had set out to find her own burial place, knowing well she would never return to the places she had left. In Texas she set up a small cemetery in a corner of her first farm, and as the family connection grew, and oddments of relations came over from Kentucky to settle, it contained at last about twenty graves. After the Grandmother's death, part of her land was to be sold for the benefit of certain of her children, and the cemetery happened to lie in the part set aside for sale. It was necessary to take up the bodies and bury them again in the family plot in the big new public cemetery, where the Grandmother had been buried. At last her husband was to lie beside her for eternity, as she had planned.

The family cemetery had been a pleasant small neglected garden of tangled rose bushes and ragged cedar trees and cypress, the simple flat stones rising out of uncropped sweet-smelling wild grass. The graves were lying open and empty one burning day when Miranda and her brother Paul, who often went together to hunt rabbits and doves, propped their twenty-two Winchester rifles carefully against the rail fence, climbed over and explored among the graves. She was nine years old and he was twelve.

They peered into the pits all shaped alike with such purposeful accuracy, and looking at each other with pleased adventurous eyes, they said in solemn tones: "These were graves!" trying by words to shape a special, suitable emotion in their minds, but they felt nothing except an agreeable thrill of wonder: they were seeing a new sight, doing something they had not done before. In them both there was also a small disappointment at the entire commonplaceness of the actual spectacle. Even if it had once contained a coffin for years upon years, when the coffin was gone a grave was just a hole in the ground. Miranda leaped into the pit that had held her grandfather's bones. Scratching around aimlessly and pleasurably as any young animal, she scooped up a lump of earth and weighed it in her palm. It had a pleasantly sweet, corrupt smell, being mixed with cedar needles and small leaves, and as the crumbs fell apart, she saw a silver dove no larger than a hazel nut, with spread wings and a neat fan-shaped tail. The breast had a deep round hollow in it. Turning it up to the fierce sunlight, she saw that the inside of the hollow was cut in little whorls. She scrambled out, over the pile of loose earth that had fallen back into one end of the grave, calling to Paul that she had found something, he must guess what . . . His head appeared smiling over the rim of another grave. He waved a closed hand at her. "I've got something too!" They ran to compare treasures, making a game of it, so many guesses each, all wrong, and a final showdown with opened palms. Paul had found a thin wide gold ring carved with intricate flowers and leaves. Miranda was smitten at sight of the ring and wished to have it. Paul seemed more impressed by the dove. They made a trade, with some little bickering. After he had got the dove in his hand, Paul said, "Don't you know what this is? This is a screw head for a *coffin!* . . . . I'll bet nobody else in the world has one like this!"

Miranda glanced at it without covetousness. She had the gold ring on her thumb; it fitted perfectly. "Maybe we ought to go now," she said, "maybe one of the niggers 'll see us and tell somebody." They knew the land had been sold, the cemetery was no longer theirs, and they felt like trespassers. They climbed back over the fence, slung their rifles loosely under their arms—they had been shooting at targets with various kinds of firearms since they were seven years old—and set out to look for the rabbits and doves or whatever small game might happen along. On these expeditions Miranda always followed at Paul's heels along the path, obeying instructions about handling her gun when going through fences; learning how to stand it up properly so it would not slip and fire unexpectedly; how to wait her time for a shot and not just bang away in the air without looking, spoiling shots for Paul, who really could hit things if given a chance. Now and then, in her excitement at seeing birds whizz up suddenly before her face, or a rabbit leap across her very toes, she lost her head, and almost without sighting she flung her rifle up and pulled the trigger. She hardly ever hit any sort of mark. She had no proper sense of hunting at all. Her brother would be often completely disgusted with her. "You don't care whether you get your bird or not," he said. "That's no way to hunt." Miranda could not understand his indignation. She had seen him smash his hat and yell with fury when he had missed his aim. "What I like about shooting," said Miranda, with exasperating inconsequence, "is pulling the trigger and hearing the noise."

"Then, by golly," said Paul, "whyn't you go back to the range and shoot at bulls-eyes?"

"I'd just as soon," said Miranda, "only like this, we walk around more."

"Well, you just stay behind and stop spoiling my shots," said Paul, who, when he made a kill, wanted to be certain he had made it. Miranda, who alone brought down a bird once in twenty rounds, always claimed as her own any game they got when they fired at the same moment. It was tiresome and unfair and her brother was sick of it.

"Now, the first dove we see, or the first rabbit, is mine," he told her. "And the next will be yours. Remember that and don't get smarty."

"What about snakes?" asked Miranda idly. "Can I have the first snake?"

Waving her thumb gently and watching her gold ring glitter, Miranda lost interest in shooting. She was wearing her summer roughing outfit: dark blue overalls, a light blue shirt, a hired-man's straw hat, and thick brown sandals. Her brother had the same outfit except his was a sober hickory-nut color. Ordinarily Miranda preferred her overalls to any other dress, though it was making rather a scandal in the countryside, for the year was 1903, and in the back country the law of female decorum had teeth in it. Her father had been criticized for letting his girls dress like boys and go careering around astride barebacked horses. Big sister Maria, the really independent and fearless one, in spite of her rather affected ways, rode at a dead run with only a rope knotted around her horse's nose. It was said the motherless family was running down, with the Grandmother no longer there to hold it together. It was known that she had discriminated against her son Harry in her will, and that he was in straits about money. Some of his old neighbors reflected with vicious satisfaction that now he would probably not be so stiffnecked, nor have any more high-stepping horses either. Miranda knew this, though she could not say how. She had met along the road old women of the kind who smoked corn-cob pipes, who had treated her grandmother with most sincere respect. They slanted their gummy old eyes side-ways at the granddaughter and said, "Ain't you ashamed of yoself, Missy? It's aginst the Scriptures to dress like that. Whut yo Pappy thinkin about?" Miranda, with her powerful social sense, which was like a fine set of antennae radiating from every pore of her skin, would feel ashamed because she knew well it was rude and ill-bred to shock anybody, even bad-tempered old crones, though she had faith in her father's judgment and was perfectly comfortable in the clothes. Her father had said, "They're just what you need, and they'll save your dresses for school. . . ." This sounded quite simple and natural to her. She had been brought up in rigorous economy. Wastefulness was vulgar. It was also a sin. These were truths; she had heard them repeated many times and never once disputed.

Now the ring, shining with the serene purity of fine gold on her rather grubby thumb, turned her feelings against her overalls and sockless feet, toes sticking through the thick brown leather straps. She wanted to go back to the farmhouse, take a good cold bath, dust herself with plenty of Maria's violet talcum powder—provided Maria was not present to object, of course—put on the thinnest, most becoming dress she owned, with a big sash, and sit in a wicker chair under the trees. . . . These things were not all she wanted, of course; she had vague stirrings of desire for luxury and a grand way of living which could not take precise form in her imagination but were founded on family legend of past wealth and leisure. These immediate comforts were what she could have, and she wanted them at once. She lagged rather far behind Paul, and once she thought of just turning back without a word and going home. She stopped, thinking that Paul would never do that to her, and so she would have to tell him. When a rabbit leaped, she let Paul have it without dispute. He killed it with one shot.

When she came up with him, he was already kneeling, examining the wound, the rabbit trailing from his hands. "Right through the head," he said complacently, as if he had aimed for it. He took out his sharp, competent bowie knife and started to skin the body. He did it very cleanly and quickly. Uncle Jimbilly knew how to prepare the skins so that Miranda always had fur coats for her dolls, for though she never cared much for her dolls she liked seeing them in fur coats. The children knelt facing each other over the dead animal. Miranda watched admiringly while her brother stripped the skin away as if he were taking off a glove. The flayed flesh emerged dark scarlet, sleek, firm; Miranda with thumb and finger felt the long fine muscles with the silvery flat strips binding them to the joints. Brother lifted the oddly bloated belly. "Look," he said, in a low amazed voice. "It was going to have young ones."

Very carefully he slit the thin flesh from the center ribs to the flanks, and a scarlet bag appeared. He slit again and pulled the bag open, and there lay a bundle of tiny rabbits, each wrapped in a thin scarlet veil. The brother pulled these off and there they were, dark gray, their sleek wet down lying in minute even ripples, like a baby's head just washed, their unbelievably small delicate ears folded close, their little blind faces almost featureless.

Miranda said, "Oh, I want to *see*," under her breath. She looked and looked—excited but not frightened, for she was accustomed to the sight of animals killed in hunting—filled with pity and astonishment and a kind of shocked delight in the won-

derful little creatures for their own sakes, they were
so pretty. She touched one of them ever so carefully. "Ah, there's blood running over them," she
said and began to tremble without knowing why.
Yet she wanted most deeply to see and to know. Having seen, she felt at once as if she had known all
along. The very memory of her former ignorance
faded, she had always known just this. No one had
ever told her anything outright, she had been rather
unobservant of the animal life around her because
she was so accustomed to animals. They seemed simply disorderly and unaccountably rude in their habits, but altogether natural and not very interesting.
Her brother had spoken as if he had known about
everything all along. He may have seen all this before. He had never said a word to her, but she knew
now a part at least of what he knew. She understood
a little of the secret, formless intuitions in her own
mind and body, which had been clearing up, taking
form, so gradually and so steadily she had not realized that she was learning what she had to know.
Paul said cautiously, as if he were talking about
something forbidden: "They were just about ready
to be born." His voice dropped on the last word. "I
know," said Miranda, "like kittens. I know, like babies." She was quietly and terribly agitated, standing again with her rifle under her arm, looking down
at the bloody heap. "I don't want the skin," she
said, "I won't have it." Paul buried the young rabbits again in their mother's body, wrapped the skin
around her, carried her to a clump of sage bushes,
and hid her away. He came out again at once and

said to Miranda, with an eager friendliness, a confidential tone quite unusual in him, as if he were taking her into an important secret on equal terms: "Listen now. Now you listen to me, and don't ever forget. Don't you ever tell a living soul that you saw this. Don't tell a soul. Don't tell Dad because I'll get into trouble. He'll say I'm leading you into things you ought not to do. He's always saying that. So now don't you go and forget and blab out sometime the way you're always doing. . . . Now, that's a secret. Don't you tell."

Miranda never told, she did not even wish to tell anybody. She thought about the whole worrisome affair with confused unhappiness for a few days. Then it sank quietly into her mind and was heaped over by accumulated thousands of impressions, for nearly twenty years. One day she was picking her path among the puddles and crushed refuse of a market street in a strange city of a strange country, when without warning, plain and clear in its true colors as if she looked through a frame upon a scene that had not stirred nor changed since the moment it happened, the episode of that far-off day leaped from its burial place before her mind's eye. She was so reasonlessly horrified she halted suddenly staring, the scene before her eyes dimmed by the vision back of them. An Indian vendor had held up before her a tray of dyed sugar sweets, in the shapes of all kinds of small creatures: birds, baby chicks, baby rabbits, lambs, baby pigs. They were in gay colors and smelled of vanilla, maybe. . . . It was a very hot day and the smell in the market, with its piles of

raw flesh and wilting flowers, was like the mingled
sweetness and corruption she had smelled that other
day in the empty cemetery at home: the day she had
remembered always until now vaguely as the time
she and her brother had found treasure in the
opened graves. Instantly upon this thought the
dreadful vision faded, and she saw clearly her
brother, whose childhood face she had forgotten,
standing again in the blazing sunshine, again twelve
years old, a pleased sober smile in his eyes, turning
the silver dove over and over in his hands.

The Jilting of
Granny Weatherall

SHE flicked her wrist neatly out of Doctor Harry's pudgy careful fingers and pulled the sheet up to her chin. The brat ought to be in knee breeches. Doctoring around the country with spectacles on his nose! "Get along now, take your schoolbooks and go. There's nothing wrong with me."

Doctor Harry spread a warm paw like a cushion on her forehead where the forked green vein danced and made her eyelids twitch. "Now, now, be a good girl, and we'll have you up in no time."

"That's no way to speak to a woman nearly eighty years old just because she's down. I'd have you respect your elders, young man."

"Well, Missy, excuse me." Doctor Harry patted her cheek. "But I've got to warn you, haven't I? You're a marvel, but you must be careful or you're going to be good and sorry."

"Don't tell me what I'm going to be. I'm on my feet now, morally speaking. It's Cornelia. I had to go to bed to get rid of her."

Her bones felt loose, and floated around in her skin, and Doctor Harry floated like a balloon around the foot of the bed. He floated and pulled down his waistcoat and swung his glasses on a cord. "Well, stay where you are, it certainly can't hurt you."

"Get along and doctor your sick," said Granny Weatherall. "Leave a well woman alone. I'll call for you when I want you. . . . Where were you forty years ago when I pulled through milk-leg and double pneumonia? You weren't even born. Don't let Cornelia lead you on," she shouted, because Doctor Harry appeared to float up to the ceiling and out. "I pay my own bills, and I don't throw my money away on nonsense!"

She meant to wave good-by, but it was too much trouble. Her eyes closed of themselves, it was like a dark curtain drawn around the bed. The pillow rose and floated under her, pleasant as a hammock in a light wind. She listened to the leaves rustling outside the window. No, somebody was swishing newspapers: no, Cornelia and Doctor Harry were whispering together. She leaped broad awake, thinking they whispered in her ear.

"She was never like this, *never* like this!" "Well, what can we expect?" "Yes, eighty years old . . ."

Well, and what if she was? She still had ears. It was like Cornelia to whisper around doors. She always kept things secret in such a public way. She was always being tactful and kind. Cornelia was dutiful; that was the trouble with her. Dutiful and good: "So good and dutiful," said Granny, "that I'd like to spank her." She saw herself spanking Cornelia and making a fine job of it.

"What'd you say, Mother?"

Granny felt her face tying up in hard knots.

"Can't a body think, I'd like to know?"

"I thought you might want something."

"I do. I want a lot of things. First off, go away and don't whisper."

She lay and drowsed, hoping in her sleep that the children would keep out and let her rest a minute. It had been a long day. Not that she was tired. It was always pleasant to snatch a minute now and then. There was always so much to be done, let me see: tomorrow.

Tomorrow was far away and there was nothing to trouble about. Things were finished somehow when the time came; thank God there was always a little margin over for peace: then a person could spread out the plan of life and tuck in the edges orderly. It was good to have everything clean and folded away, with the hair brushes and tonic bottles sitting straight on the white embroidered linen: the day started without fuss and the pantry shelves laid out with rows of jelly glasses and brown jugs and white stone-china jars with blue whirligigs and words painted on them: coffee, tea, sugar, ginger, cinnamon, allspice: and the bronze clock with the lion on top nicely dusted off. The dust that lion could collect in twenty-four hours! The box in the attic with all those letters tied up, well, she'd have to go through that tomorrow. All those letters—George's letters and John's letters and her letters to them both—lying around for the children to find afterwards made her uneasy. Yes, that would be tomorrow's business. No use to let them know how silly she had been once.

While she was rummaging around she found death in her mind and it felt clammy and unfamiliar. She had spent so much time preparing for death there was no need for bringing it up again. Let it take care of itself now. When she was sixty she had felt very old, finished, and went around making farewell trips to see her children and grandchildren, with a secret in her mind: This is the very last of your mother, children! Then she made her will and came down with a long fever. That was all just a notion like a lot of other things, but it was lucky too, for she had once for all got over the idea of dying for a long time. Now she couldn't be worried. She hoped she had better sense now. Her father had lived to be one hundred and two years old and had drunk a noggin of strong hot toddy on his last birthday. He told the reporters it was his daily habit, and he owed his long life to that. He had made quite a scandal and was very pleased about it. She believed she'd just plague Cornelia a little.

"Cornelia! Cornelia!" No footsteps, but a sudden hand on her cheek. "Bless you, where have you been?"

"Here, Mother."

"Well, Cornelia, I want a noggin of hot toddy."

"Are you cold, darling?"

"I'm chilly, Cornelia. Lying in bed stops the circulation. I must have told you that a thousand times."

Well, she could just hear Cornelia telling her husband that Mother was getting a little childish and they'd have to humor her. The thing that most annoyed her was that Cornelia thought she was deaf, dumb, and blind. Little hasty glances and tiny gestures tossed around her and over her head saying, "Don't cross her, let her have her way, she's eighty years old," and she sitting there as if she lived in a thin glass cage. Sometimes Granny almost made up her mind to pack up and move back to her own house where nobody could remind her every minute that she was old. Wait, wait, Cornelia, till your own children whisper behind your back!

In her day she had kept a better house and had got more work done. She wasn't too old yet for Lydia to be driving eighty miles for advice when one of the children jumped the track, and Jimmy still dropped in and talked things over: "Now, Mammy, you've a good business head, I want to know what you think of this? . . ." Old. Cornelia couldn't change the furniture around without asking. Little things, little things! They had been so sweet when they were little. Granny wished the old days were back again with the children young and everything to be done over. It had been a hard pull, but not too much for her. When she thought of all the food she had cooked, and all the clothes she had cut and sewed, and all the gardens she had made—well, the children showed it. There they were, made out of her, and they couldn't get away from that. Sometimes she wanted to see John again and point to them and say, Well, I didn't do so badly, did I? But that would have to wait. That was for tomorrow. She used to think of him as a man, but now all the children were older than their father, and he would be a child beside her if she saw him now. It seemed strange and there was something wrong in the idea. Why, he couldn't possibly recognize her. She had fenced in a hundred acres once, digging the post holes herself and clamping the wires with just a Negro boy to help. That changed a woman. John would be looking for a young woman with the peaked Spanish comb in her hair and the painted fan. Digging post holes changed a woman. Riding country roads in the winter when women had their babies was another thing: sitting up nights with sick horses and sick Negroes and sick children and hardly ever losing one. John, I hardly ever lost one of them! John would see that in a minute, that would be something he could understand, she wouldn't have to explain anything!

It made her feel like rolling up her sleeves and putting the whole place to rights again. No matter if Cornelia was determined to be everywhere at once, there were a great many things left undone on this place. She would start tomorrow and do them. It was good to be strong enough for everything, even if all you made melted and changed and slipped under your hands, so that by the time you finished you almost forgot what you were working for. What was it I set out to do? she asked herself intently, but she could not remember. A fog rose over the valley, she saw it marching across the creek swallowing the trees and moving up the hill like an army of ghosts. Soon it would be at the near edge of the orchard, and then it was time to go in and light the lamps. Come in, children, don't stay out in the night air.

Lighting the lamps had been beautiful. The children huddled up to her and breathed like little calves waiting at the bars in the twilight. Their eyes followed the match and watched the flame rise and settle in a blue curve, then they moved away from her. The lamp was lit, they didn't have to be scared and hang on to mother any more. Never, never, never more. God, for all my life I thank Thee. Without Thee, my God, I could never have done it. Hail, Mary, full of grace.

I want you to pick all the fruit this year and see that nothing is wasted. There's always someone who can use it. Don't let good things rot for want of using. You waste life when you waste good food. Don't let things get lost. It's bitter to lose things. Now, don't let me get to thinking, not when I am tired and taking a little nap before supper. . . .

The pillow rose about her shoulders and pressed against her heart and the memory was being squeezed out of it: oh, push down the pillow, somebody: it would smother her if she tried to hold it. Such a fresh breeze blowing and such a green day with no threats in it. But he had not come, just the same. What does a woman do when she has put on the white veil and set out the white cake for a man and he doesn't come? She tried to remember. No, I swear he never harmed me but in that. He never harmed me but in that . . . and what if he did? There was the day, the day, but a whirl of dark smoke rose and covered it, crept up and over into the bright field where everything was planted so carefully in orderly rows. That was hell, she knew hell when she saw it.

For sixty years she had prayed against remembering him and against losing her soul in the deep pit
of hell, and now the two things were mingled in one
and the thought of him was a smoky cloud from hell
that moved and crept in her head when she had just
got rid of Doctor Harry and was trying to rest a
minute. Wounded vanity, Ellen, said a sharp voice
in the top of her mind. Don't let your wounded
vanity get the upper hand of you. Plenty of girls
get jilted. You were jilted, weren't you? Then stand
up to it. Her eyelids wavered and let in streamers
of blue-gray light like tissue paper over her eyes.
She must get up and pull the shades down or she'd
never sleep. She was in bed again and the shades
were not down. How could that happen? Better turn
over, hide from the light, sleeping in the light gave
you nightmares. "Mother, how do you feel now?"
and a stinging wetness on her forehead. But I don't
like having my face washed in cold water!

Hapsy? George? Lydia? Jimmy? No, Cornelia,
and her features were swollen and full of little puddles. "They're coming, darling, they'll all be here
soon." Go wash your face, child, you look funny.

Instead of obeying, Cornelia knelt down and put
her head on the pillow. She seemed to be talking
but there was no sound. "Well, are you tongue-tied?
Whose birthday is it? Are you going to give a
party?"

Cornelia's mouth moved urgently in strange
shapes. "Don't do that, you bother me, daughter."

"Oh, no, Mother. Oh, no . . ."

Nonsense. It was strange about children. They

72

disputed your every word. "No what, Cornelia?"

"Here's Doctor Harry."

"I won't see that boy again. He just left five minutes ago."

"That was this morning, Mother. It's night now. Here's the nurse."

"This is Doctor Harry, Mrs. Weatherall. I never saw you look so young and happy!"

"Ah, I'll never be young again—but I'd be happy if they'd let me lie in peace and get rested."

She thought she spoke up loudly, but no one answered. A warm weight on her forehead, a warm bracelet on her wrist, and a breeze went on whispering, trying to tell her something. A shuffle of leaves in the everlasting hand of God, He blew on them and they danced and rattled. "Mother, don't mind, we're going to give you a little hypodermic." "Look here, daughter, how do ants get in this bed? I saw sugar ants yesterday." Did you send for Hapsy too?

It was Hapsy she really wanted. She had to go a long way back through a great many rooms to find Hapsy standing with a baby on her arm. She seemed to herself to be Hapsy also, and the baby on Hapsy's arm was Hapsy and himself and herself, all at once, and there was no surprise in the meeting. Then Hapsy melted from within and turned flimsy as gray gauze and the baby was a gauzy shadow, and Hapsy came up close and said, "I thought you'd never come," and looked at her very searchingly and said, "You haven't changed a bit!" They leaned forward to kiss, when Cornelia began whispering from a long way off, "Oh, is there anything you

73

want to tell me? Is there anything I can do for you?"

Yes, she had changed her mind after sixty years and she would like to see George. I want you to find George. Find him and be sure to tell him I forgot him. I want him to know I had my husband just the same and my children and my house like any other woman. A good house too and a good husband that I loved and fine children out of him. Better than I hoped for even. Tell him I was given back everything he took away and more. Oh, no, oh, God, no, there was something else besides the house and the man and the children. Oh, surely they were not all? What was it? Something not given back. . . . Her breath crowded down under her ribs and grew into a monstrous frightening shape with cutting edges; it bored up into her head, and the agony was unbelievable: Yes, John, get the doctor now, no more talk, my time has come.

When this one was born it should be the last. The last. It should have been born first, for it was the one she had truly wanted. Everything came in good time. Nothing left out, left over. She was strong, in three days she would be as well as ever. Better. A woman needed milk in her to have her full health.

"Mother, do you hear me?"

"I've been telling you—"

"Mother, Father Connolly's here."

"I went to Holy Communion only last week. Tell him I'm not so sinful as all that."

"Father just wants to speak to you."

He could speak as much as he pleased. It was like

him to drop in and inquire about her soul as if it were a teething baby, and then stay on for a cup of tea and a round of cards and gossip. He always had a funny story of some sort, usually about an Irishman who made his little mistakes and confessed them, and the point lay in some absurd thing he would blurt out in the confessional showing his struggles between native piety and original sin. Granny felt easy about her soul. Cornelia, where are your manners? Give Father Connolly a chair. She had her secret comfortable understanding with a few favorite saints who cleared a straight road to God for her. All as surely signed and sealed as the papers for the new Forty Acres. Forever . . . heirs and assigns forever. Since the day the wedding cake was not cut, but thrown out and wasted. The whole bottom dropped out of the world, and there she was blind and sweating with nothing under her feet and the walls falling away. His hand had caught her under the breast, she had not fallen, there was the freshly polished floor with the green rug on it, just as before. He had cursed like a sailor's parrot and said, "I'll kill him for you." Don't lay a hand on him, for my sake leave something to God. "Now, Ellen, you must believe what I tell you. . . ."

So there was nothing, nothing to worry about any more, except sometimes in the night one of the children screamed in a nightmare, and they both hustled out shaking and hunting for the matches and calling, "There, wait a minute, here we are!" John, get the doctor now, Hapsy's time has come But there was Hapsy standing by the bed in a white cap. "Cornelia, tell Hapsy to take off her cap. I can't see her plain."

Her eyes opened very wide and the room stood out like a picture she had seen somewhere. Dark colors with the shadows rising toward the ceiling in long angles. The tall black dresser gleamed with nothing on it but John's picture, enlarged from a little one, with John's eyes very black when they should have been blue. You never saw him, so how do you know how he looked? But the man insisted the copy was perfect, it was very rich and handsome. For a picture, yes, but it's not my husband. The table by the bed had a linen cover and a candle and a crucifix. The light was blue from Cornelia's silk lampshades. No sort of light at all, just frippery. You had to live forty years with kerosene lamps to appreciate honest electricity. She felt very strong and she saw Doctor Harry with a rosy nimbus around him.

"You look like a saint, Doctor Harry, and I vow that's as near as you'll ever come to it."

"She's saying something."

"I heard you, Cornelia. What's all this carrying-on?"

"Father Connolly's saying—"

Cornelia's voice staggered and bumped like a cart in a bad road. It rounded corners and turned back again and arrived nowhere. Granny stepped up in the cart very lightly and reached for the reins, but a man sat beside her and she knew him by his hands, driving the cart. She did not look in his face, for she knew without seeing, but looked instead down the road where the trees leaned over and bowed to each other and a thousand birds were singing a Mass. She felt like singing too, but she put her hand in the bosom of her dress and pulled out a rosary, and Father Connolly murmured Latin in a very solemn voice and tickled her feet. My God, will you stop that nonsense? I'm a married woman. What if he did run away and leave me to face the priest by myself? I found another a whole world better. I wouldn't have exchanged my husband for anybody except Saint Michael himself, and you may tell him that for me with a thank you in the bargain.

Light flashed on her closed eyelids, and a deep roaring shook her. Cornelia, is that lightning? I hear thunder. There's going to be a storm. Close all the windows. Call the children in. . . . "Mother, here we are, all of us." "Is that you, Hapsy?" "Oh, no, I'm Lydia. We drove as fast as we could." Their faces drifted above her, drifted away. The rosary fell out of her hands and Lydia put it back. Jimmy tried to help, their hands fumbled together, and Granny closed two fingers around Jimmy's thumb. Beads wouldn't do, it must be something alive. She was so amazed her thoughts ran round and round. So, my dear Lord, this is my death and I wasn't even thinking about it. My children have come to see me die. But I can't, it's not time. Oh, I always hated surprises. I wanted to give Cornelia the amethyst set —Cornelia, you're to have the amethyst set, but Hapsy's to wear it when she wants, and, Doctor Harry, do shut up. Nobody sent for you. Oh, my dear Lord, do wait a minute. I meant to do something about the Forty Acres, Jimmy doesn't need it and Lydia will later on, with that worthless husband of hers. I meant to finish the altar cloth and send six bottles of wine to Sister Borgia for her dyspepsia. I want to send six bottles of wine to Sister Borgia, Father Connolly, now don't let me forget.

Cornelia's voice made short turns and tilted over and crashed. "Oh, Mother, oh, Mother, oh, Mother . . ."

"I'm not going, Cornelia. I'm taken by surprise. I can't go."

You'll see Hapsy again. What about her? "I thought you'd never come." Granny made a long journey outward, looking for Hapsy. What if I don't find her? What then? Her heart sank down and down, there was no bottom to death, she couldn't come to the end of it. The blue light from Cornelia's lampshade drew into a tiny point in the center of her brain, it flickered and winked like an eye, quietly it fluttered and dwindled. Granny lay curled down within herself, amazed and watchful, staring at the point of light that was herself; her body was now only a deeper mass of shadow in an endless darkness and this darkness would curl around the light and swallow it up. God, give a sign!

For the second time there was no sign. Again no bridegroom and the priest in the house. She could not remember any other sorrow because this grief wiped them all away. Oh, no, there's nothing more cruel than this—I'll never forgive it. She stretched herself with a deep breath and blew out the light.

He

Lᴵꜰᴇ was very hard for the Whipples. It was hard to feed all the hungry mouths, it was hard to keep the children in flannels during the winter, short as it was: "God knows what would become of us if we lived north," they would say: keeping them decently clean was hard. "It looks like our luck won't never let up on us," said Mr. Whipple, but Mrs. Whipple was all for taking what was sent and calling it good, anyhow when the neighbors were in earshot. "Don't ever let a soul hear us complain," she kept saying to her husband. She couldn't stand to be pitied. "No, not if it comes to it that we have to live in a wagon and pick cotton around the country," she said, "nobody's going to get a chance to look down on us."

Mrs. Whipple loved her second son, the simpleminded one, better than she loved the other two children put together. She was forever saying so, and when she talked with certain of her neighbors, she would even throw in her husband and her mother for good measure.

"You needn't keep on saying it around," said Mr.

Whipple, "you'll make people think nobody else has any feelings about Him but you."

"It's natural for a mother," Mrs. Whipple would remind him. "You know yourself it's more natural for a mother to be that way. People don't expect so much of fathers, some way."

This didn't keep the neighbors from talking plainly among themselves. "A Lord's pure mercy if He should die," they said. "It's the sins of the fathers," they agreed among themselves. "There's bad blood and bad doings somewhere, you can bet on that." This behind the Whipples' backs. To their faces everybody said, "He's not so bad off. He'll be all right yet. Look how He grows!"

Mrs. Whipple hated to talk about it, she tried to keep her mind off it, but every time anybody set foot in the house, the subject always came up, and she had to talk about Him first, before she could get on to anything else. It seemed to ease her mind. "I wouldn't have anything happen to Him for all the world, but it just looks like I can't keep Him out of mischief. He's so strong and active, He's always into everything; He was like that since He could walk. It's actually funny sometimes, the way He can do anything; it's laughable to see Him up to His tricks. Emly has more accidents; I'm forever tying up her bruises, and Adna can't fall a foot without cracking a bone. But He can do anything and not get a scratch. The preacher said such a nice thing once when he was here. He said, and I'll remember it to my dying day, 'The innocent walk with God—that's why He don't get hurt.'" Whenever Mrs. Whipple repeated these words, she always felt a warm pool spread in her breast, and the tears would fill her eyes, and then she could talk about something else.

He did grow and He never got hurt. A plank blew off the chicken house and struck Him on the head and He never seemed to know it. He had learned a few words, and after this He forgot them. He didn't whine for food as the other children did, but waited until it was given Him; He ate squatting in the corner, smacking and mumbling. Rolls of fat covered Him like an overcoat, and He could carry twice as much wood and water as Adna. Emly had a cold in the head most of the time—"she takes that after me," said Mrs. Whipple—so in bad weather they gave her the extra blanket off His cot. He never seemed to mind the cold.

Just the same, Mrs. Whipple's life was a torment for fear something might happen to Him. He climbed the peach trees much better than Adna and went skittering along the branches like a monkey, just a regular monkey. "Oh, Mrs. Whipple, you hadn't ought to let Him do that. He'll lose His balance sometime. He can't rightly know what He's doing."

Mrs. Whipple almost screamed out at the neighbor. "He *does* know what He's doing! He's as able as any other child! Come down out of there, you!" When He finally reached the ground she could hardly keep her hands off Him for acting like that before people, a grin all over His face and her worried sick about Him all the time.

"It's the neighbors," said Mrs. Whipple to her husband. "Oh, I do mortally wish they would keep out of our business. I can't afford to let Him do anything for fear they'll come nosing around about it. Look at the bees, now. Adna can't handle them, they sting him up so; I haven't got time to do everything, and now I don't dare let Him. But if He gets a sting He don't really mind."

"It's just because He ain't got sense enough to be scared of anything," said Mr. Whipple.

"You ought to be ashamed of yourself," said Mrs. Whipple, "talking that way about your own child. Who's to take up for Him if we don't, I'd like to know? He sees a lot that goes on, He listens to things all the time. And anything I tell Him to do He does it. Don't never let anybody hear you say such things. They'd think you favored the other children over Him."

"Well, now I don't, and you know it, and what's the use of getting all worked up about it? You always think the worst of everything. Just let Him alone, He'll get along somehow. He gets plenty to eat and wear, don't He?" Mr. Whipple suddenly felt tired out. "Anyhow, it can't be helped now."

Mrs. Whipple felt tired too, she complained in a tired voice. "What's done can't never be undone, I know that good as anybody; but He's my child, and I'm not going to have people say anything. I get sick of people coming around saying things all the time."

In the early fall Mrs. Whipple got a letter from her brother saying he and his wife and two children were coming over for a little visit next Sunday week. "Put the big pot in the little one," he wrote at the

84

end. Mrs. Whipple read this part out loud twice, she was so pleased. Her brother was a great one for saying funny things. "We'll just show him that's no joke," she said, "we'll just butcher one of the sucking pigs."

"It's a waste and I don't hold with waste the way we are now," said Mr. Whipple. "That pig'll be worth money by Christmas."

"It's a shame and a pity we can't have a decent meal's vittles once in a while when my own family comes to see us," said Mrs. Whipple. "I'd hate for his wife to go back and say there wasn't a thing in the house to eat. My God, it's better than buying up a great chance of meat in town. There's where you'd spend the money!"

"All right, do it yourself then," said Mr. Whipple. "Christamighty, no wonder we can't get ahead!"

The question was how to get the little pig away from his ma, a great fighter, worse than a Jersey cow. Adna wouldn't try it: "That sow'd rip my insides out all over the pen." "All right, old fraidy," said Mrs. Whipple, "*He's* not scared. Watch *Him* do it." And she laughed as though it was all a good joke and gave Him a little push toward the pen. He sneaked up and snatched the pig right away from the teat and galloped back and was over the fence with the sow raging at His heels. The little black squirming thing was screeching like a baby in a tantrum, stiffening its back and stretching its mouth to the ears. Mrs. Whipple took the pig with her face stiff and sliced its throat with one stroke. When He saw the blood He gave a great jolting breath and ran away. "But He'll forget and eat plenty, just the same," thought Mrs. Whipple. Whenever she was thinking, her lips moved making words. "He'd eat it all if I didn't stop Him. He'd eat up every mouthful from the other two if I'd let Him."

She felt badly about it. He was ten years old now and a third again as large as Adna, who was going on fourteen. "It's a shame, a shame," she kept saying under her breath, "and Adna with so much brains!"

She kept on feeling badly about all sorts of things. In the first place it was the man's work to butcher; the sight of the pig scraped pink and naked made her sick. He was too fat and soft and pitiful-looking. It was simply a shame the way things had to happen. By the time she had finished it up, she almost wished her brother would stay at home.

Early Sunday morning Mrs. Whipple dropped everything to get Him all cleaned up. In an hour He was dirty again, with crawling under fences after a possum, and straddling along the rafters of the barn looking for eggs in the hayloft. "My Lord, look at you now after all my trying! And here's Adna and Emly staying so quiet. I get tired trying to keep you decent. Get off that shirt and put on another, people will say I don't half dress you!" And she boxed Him on the ears, hard. He blinked and blinked and rubbed His head, and His face hurt Mrs. Whipple's feelings. Her knees began to tremble, she had to sit down while she buttoned His shirt. "I'm just all gone before the day starts."

The brother came with his plump healthy wife and two great roaring hungry boys. They had a grand dinner, with the pig roasted to a crackling in the middle of the table, full of dressing, a pickled peach in his mouth and plenty of gravy for the sweet potatoes.

"This looks like prosperity all right," said the brother; "you're going to have to roll me home like I was a barrel when I'm done."

Everybody laughed out loud; it was fine to hear them laughing all at once around the table. Mrs. Whipple felt warm and good about it. "Oh, we've got six more of these; I say it's as little as we can do when you come to see us so seldom."

He wouldn't come into the dining room, and Mrs. Whipple passed it off very well. "He's timider than my other two," she said, "He'll just have to get used to you. There isn't everybody He'll make up with, you know how it is with some children, even cousins." Nobody said anything out of the way.

"Just like my Alfy here," said the brother's wife. "I sometimes got to lick him to make him shake hands with his own grand-mammy."

So that was over, and Mrs. Whipple loaded up a big plate for Him first, before everybody. "I always say He ain't to be slighted, no matter who else goes without," she said, and carried it to Him herself.

"He can chin Himself on the top of the door," said Emly, helping along.

"That's fine, He's getting along fine," said the brother.

They went away after supper. Mrs. Whipple rounded up the dishes, and sent the children to bed and sat down and unlaced her shoes. "You see?" she said to Mr. Whipple. "That's the way my whole family is. Nice and considerate about everything. No out-of-the-way remarks—they *have* got refinement. I get awfully sick of people's remarks. Wasn't that pig good?"

Mr. Whipple said, "Yes, we're out three hundred pounds of pork, that's all. It's easy to be polite when you come to eat. Who knows what they had in their minds all along?"

"Yes, that's like you," said Mrs. Whipple. "I don't expect anything else from you. You'll be telling me next that my own brother will be saying around that we made Him eat in the kitchen! Oh, my God!" She rocked her head in her hands, a hard pain started in the very middle of her forehead. "Now it's all spoiled, and everything was so nice and easy. All right, you don't like them and you never did—all right, they'll not come here again soon, never you mind! But they *can't* say He wasn't dressed every lick as good as Adna—oh, honest, sometimes I wish I was dead!"

"I wish you'd let up," said Mr. Whipple. "It's bad enough as it is."

It was a hard winter. It seemed to Mrs. Whipple that they hadn't ever known anything but hard times, and now to cap it all a winter like this. The crops were about half of what they had a right to expect; after the cotton was in it didn't do much more than cover the grocery bill. They swapped off one of the plow horses, and got cheated, for the new one died of the heaves. Mrs. Whipple kept thinking all the time it was terrible to have a man you couldn't depend on not to get cheated. They cut down on everything, but Mrs. Whipple kept saying there are things you can't cut down on, and they cost money. It took a lot of warm clothes for Adna and Emly, who walked four miles to school during the three-months session. "He sets around the fire a lot, He won't need so much," said Mr. Whipple. "That's so," said Mrs. Whipple, "and when He does the outdoor chores He can wear your tarpaullion coat. I can't do no better, that's all."

In February He was taken sick, and lay curled up under His blanket looking very blue in the face and acting as if He would choke. Mr. and Mrs. Whipple did everything they could for Him for two days, and then they were scared and sent for the doctor. The doctor told them they must keep Him warm and give Him plenty of milk and eggs. "He isn't as stout as He looks, I'm afraid," said the doctor. "You've got to watch them when they're like that. You must put more cover onto Him, too."

"I just took off His big blanket to wash," said Mrs. Whipple, ashamed. "I can't stand dirt."

"Well, you'd better put it back on the minute it's dry," said the doctor, "or He'll have pneumonia."

Mr. and Mrs. Whipple took a blanket off their own bed and put His cot in by the fire. "They can't say we didn't do everything for Him," she said, "even to sleeping cold ourselves on His account."

When the winter broke He seemed to be well again, but He walked as if His feet hurt Him. He was able to run a cotton planter during the season.

"I got it all fixed up with Jim Ferguson about breeding the cow next time," said Mr. Whipple. "I'll pasture the bull this summer and give Jim some fodder in the fall. That's better than paying out money when you haven't got it."

"I hope you didn't say such a thing before Jim Ferguson," said Mrs. Whipple. "You oughtn't to let him know we're so down as all that."

"Godamighty, that ain't saying we're down. A man is got to look ahead sometimes. *He* can lead the bull over today. I need Adna on the place."

At first Mrs. Whipple felt easy in her mind about sending Him for the bull. Adna was too jumpy and couldn't be trusted. You've got to be steady around animals. After He was gone she started thinking, and after a while she could hardly bear it any longer. She stood in the lane and watched for Him. It was nearly three miles to go and a hot day, but He oughtn't to be so long about it. She shaded her eyes and stared until colored bubbles floated in her eyeballs. It was just like everything else in life, she must always worry and never know a moment's peace about anything. After a long time she saw Him turn into the side lane, limping. He came on very slowly, leading the big hulk of an animal by a ring in the nose, twirling a little stick in His hand, never looking back or sideways, but coming on like a sleep-walker with His eyes half shut.

Mrs. Whipple was scared sick of bulls; she had

heard awful stories about how they followed on quietly enough, and then suddenly pitched on with a bellow and pawed and gored a body to pieces. Any second now that black monster would come down on Him, my God, He'd never have sense enough to run.

She mustn't make a sound nor a move; she mustn't get the bull started. The bull heaved his head aside and horned the air at a fly. Her voice burst out of her in a shriek, and she screamed at Him to come on, for God's sake. He didn't seem to hear her clamor, but kept on twirling His switch and limping on, and the bull lumbered along behind him as gently as a calf. Mrs. Whipple stopped calling and ran toward the house, praying under her breath: "Lord, don't let anything happen to Him. Lord, you *know* people will say we oughtn't to have sent Him. You *know* they'll say we didn't take care of Him. Oh, get Him home, safe home, safe home, and I'll look out for Him better! Amen."

She watched from the window while He led the beast in, and tied him up in the barn. It was no use trying to keep up, Mrs. Whipple couldn't bear another thing. She sat down and rocked and cried with her apron over her head.

From year to year the Whipples were growing poorer and poorer. The place just seemed to run down of itself, no matter how hard they worked. "We're losing our hold," said Mrs. Whipple. "Why can't we do like other people and watch for our best chances? They'll be calling us poor white trash next."

"When I get to be sixteen I'm going to leave,"

said Adna. "I'm going to get a job in Powell's grocery store. There's money in that. No more farm for me."

"I'm going to be a schoolteacher," said Emly. "But I've got to finish the eighth grade, anyhow. Then I can live in town. I don't see any chances here."

"Emly takes after my family," said Mrs. Whipple. "Ambitious every last one of them, and they don't take second place for anybody."

When fall came Emly got a chance to wait on table in the railroad eating-house in the town near by, and it seemed such a shame not to take it when the wages were good and she could get her food too, that Mrs. Whipple decided to let her take it, and not bother with school until the next session. "You've got plenty of time," she said. "You're young and smart as a whip."

With Adna gone too, Mr. Whipple tried to run the farm with just Him to help. He seemed to get along fine, doing His work and part of Adna's without noticing it. They did well enough until Christmas time, when one morning He slipped on the ice coming up from the barn. Instead of getting up He thrashed round and round, and when Mr. Whipple got to Him, He was having some sort of fit.

They brought Him inside and tried to make Him sit up, but He blubbered and rolled, so they put Him to bed and Mr. Whipple rode to town for the doctor. All the way there and back he worried about where the money was to come from: it sure did look like he had about all the troubles he could carry.

From then on He stayed in bed. His legs swelled up double their size, and the fits kept coming back. After four months, the doctor said, "It's no use, I think you'd better put Him in the County Home for treatment right away. I'll see about it for you. He'll have good care there and be off your hands."

"We don't begrudge Him any care, and I won't let Him out of my sight," said Mrs. Whipple. "I won't have it said I sent my sick child off among strangers."

"I know how you feel," said the doctor. "You can't tell me anything about that, Mrs. Whipple. I've got a boy of my own. But you'd better listen to me. I can't do anything more for Him, that's the truth."

Mr. and Mrs. Whipple talked it over a long time that night after they went to bed. "It's just charity," said Mrs. Whipple, "that's what we've come to, charity! I certainly never looked for this."

"We pay taxes to help support the place just like everybody else," said Mr. Whipple, "and I don't call that taking charity. I think it would be fine to have Him where He'd get the best of everything . . . and besides, I can't keep up with these doctor bills any longer."

"Maybe that's why the doctor wants us to send Him—he's scared he won't get his money," said Mrs. Whipple.

"Don't talk like that," said Mr. Whipple, feeling pretty sick, "or we won't be able to send Him."

"Oh, but we won't keep Him there long," said Mrs. Whipple. "Soon's He's better, we'll bring Him right back home."

"The doctor has told you and told you time and again He can't ever get better, and you might as well stop talking," said Mr. Whipple.

"Doctors don't know everything," said Mrs. Whipple, feeling almost happy. "But anyhow, in the summer Emly can come home for a vacation, and Adna can get down for Sundays: we'll all work together and get on our feet again, and the children will feel they've got a place to come to."

All at once she saw it full summer again, with the garden going fine, and new white roller shades up all over the house, and Adna and Emly home, so full of life, all of them happy together. Oh, it could happen, things would ease up on them.

They didn't talk before Him much, but they never knew just how much He understood. Finally the doctor set the day and a neighbor who owned a double-seated carry-all offered to drive them over. The hospital would have sent an ambulance, but Mrs. Whipple couldn't stand to see Him going away looking so sick as all that. They wrapped Him in blankets, and the neighbor and Mr. Whipple lifted Him into the back seat of the carry-all beside Mrs. Whipple, who had on her black shirtwaist. She couldn't stand to go looking like charity.

"You'll be all right, I guess I'll stay behind," said Mr. Whipple. "It don't look like everybody ought to leave the place at once."

"Besides, it ain't as if He was going to stay forever," said Mrs. Whipple to the neighbor. "This is only for a little while."

They started away, Mrs. Whipple holding to the edges of the blankets to keep Him from sagging sideways. He sat there blinking and blinking. He worked His hands out and began rubbing His nose with His knuckles, and then with the end of the blanket. Mrs. Whipple couldn't believe what she saw; He was scrubbing away big tears that rolled out of the corners of His eyes. He sniveled and made a gulping noise. Mrs. Whipple kept saying, "Oh, honey, you don't feel so bad, do you? You don't feel so bad, do you?" for He seemed to be accusing her of something. Maybe He remembered that time she boxed His ears, maybe He had been scared that day with the bull, maybe He had slept cold and couldn't tell her about it; maybe He knew they were sending Him away for good and all because they were too poor to keep Him. Whatever it was, Mrs. Whipple couldn't bear to think of it. She began to cry, frightfully, and wrapped her arms tight around Him. His head rolled on her shoulder: she had loved Him as much as she possibly could, there were Adna and Emly who had to be thought of too, there was nothing she could do to make up to Him for His life. Oh, what a mortal pity He was ever born.

They came in sight of the hospital, with the neighbor driving very fast, not daring to look behind him.

Magic

And, Madame Blanchard, believe that I am happy to be here with you and your family because it is so serene, everything, and before this I worked for a long time in a fancy house—maybe you don't know what is a fancy house? Naturally . . . everyone must have heard sometime or other. Well, Madame, I work always where there is work to be had, and so in this place I worked very hard all hours, and saw too many things, things you wouldn't believe, and I wouldn't think of telling you, only maybe it will rest you while I brush your hair. You'll excuse me too but I could not help hearing you say to the laundress maybe someone had bewitched your linens, they fall away so fast in the wash. Well, there was a girl there in that house, a poor thing, thin, but well-liked by all the men who called, and you understand she could not get along with the woman who ran the house. They quarreled, the madam cheated her on her checks: you know, the girl got a check, a brass one, every time, and at the week's end she gave those back to the madam, yes, that was the way, and got her percentage, a very small little of her earnings: it is a business, you

99

see, like any other—and the madam used to pretend the girl had given back only so many checks, you see, and really she had given many more, but after they were out of her hands, what could she do? So she would say, I will get out of this place, and curse and cry. Then the madam would hit her over the head. She always hit people over the head with bottles, it was the way she fought. My good heavens, Madame Blanchard, what confusion there would be sometimes with a girl running raving downstairs, and the madam pulling her back by the hair and smashing a bottle on her forehead.

It was nearly always about the money, the girls got in debt so, and if they wished to go they could not without paying every sou marqué. The madam had full understanding with the police; the girls must come back with them or go to the jails. Well, they always came back with the policemen or with another kind of man friend of the madam: she could make men work for her too, but she paid them very well for all, let me tell you: and so the girls stayed on unless they were sick; if so, if they got too sick, she sent them away again.

Madame Blanchard said, "You are pulling a little here," and eased a strand of hair: "and then what?"

Pardon—but this girl, there was a true hatred between her and the madam. She would say many times, I make more money than anybody else in the house, and every week were scenes. So at last she said one morning, Now I will leave this place, and she took out forty dollars from under her pillow and said, Here's your money! The madam began to shout, Where did you get all that, you ——? and accused her of robbing the men who came to visit her. The girl said, Keep your hands off or I'll brain you: and at that the madam took hold of her shoulders, and began to lift her knee and kick this girl most terribly in the stomach, and even in her most secret place, Madame Blanchard, and then she beat her in the face with a bottle, and the girl fell back again into her room where I was making clean. I helped her to the bed, and she sat there holding her sides with her head hanging down, and when she got up again there was blood everywhere she had sat. So then the madam came in once more and screamed, Now you can get out, you are no good for me any more: I don't repeat all, you understand it is too much. But she took all the money she could find, and at the door she gave the girl a great push in the back with her knee, so that she fell again in the street, and then got up and went away with the dress barely on her.

After this the men who knew this girl kept saying, Where is Ninette? And they kept asking this in the next days, so that the madam could not say any longer, I put her out because she is a thief. No, she began to see she was wrong to send this Ninette away, and then she said, She will be back in a few days, don't trouble yourself.

And now, Madame Blanchard, if you wish to hear, I come to the strange part, the thing recalled to me when you said your linens were bewitched. For the cook in that place was a woman, colored like myself, like myself with much French blood just the same, like myself living always among people who worked spells. But she had a very hard heart, she helped the madam in everything, she liked to watch all that happened, and she gave away tales on the girls. The madam trusted her above everything, and she said, Well, where can I find that slut? because she had gone altogether out of Basin Street before the madam began to ask the police to bring her again. Well, the cook said, I know a charm that works here in New Orleans, colored women do it to bring back their men: in seven days they come again very happy to stay and they cannot say why: even your enemy will come back to you believing you are his friend. It is a New Orleans charm for sure, for certain, they say it does not work even across the river. . . . And then they did it just as the cook said. They took the chamber pot of this girl from under her bed, and in it they mixed with water and milk all the relics of her they found there: the hair from her brush, and the face powder from the puff, and even little bits of her nails they found about the edges of the carpet where she sat by habit to cut her finger- and toe-nails; and they dipped the sheets with her blood into the water, and all the time the cook said something over it in a low voice; I could not hear all, but at last she said to the madam, Now spit in it: and the madam spat, and the cook said, When she comes back she will be dirt under your feet.

Madame Blanchard closed her perfume bottle with a thin click: "Yes, and then?"

Then in seven nights the girl came back and she looked very sick, the same clothes and all, but happy

to be there. One of the men said, Welcome home,
Ninette! and when she started to speak to the
madam, the madam said, Shut up and get upstairs
and dress yourself. So Ninette, this girl, she said,
I'll be down in just a minute. And after that she
lived there quietly.

Old Mortality

Part I: 1885-1902

SHE was a spirited-looking young woman, with dark curly hair cropped and parted on the side, a short oval face with straight eyebrows, and a large curved mouth. A round white collar rose from the neck of her tightly buttoned black basque, and round white cuffs set off lazy hands with dimples in them, lying at ease in the folds of her flounced skirt which gathered around to a bustle. She sat thus, forever in the pose of being photographed, a motionless image in her dark walnut frame with silver oak leaves in the corners, her smiling gray eyes following one about the room. It was a reckless indifferent smile, rather disturbing to her nieces Maria and Miranda. Quite often they wondered why every older person who looked at the picture said, "How lovely"; and why everyone who had known her thought her so beautiful and charming.

There was a kind of faded merriment in the background, with its vase of flowers and draped velvet curtains, the kind of vase and the kind of curtains no one would have any more. The clothes were not even romantic looking, but merely most terribly out of fashion, and the whole affair was associated, in the minds of the little girls, with dead things: the smell of Grandmother's medicated cigarettes and her furniture that smelled of beeswax, and her old-fashioned perfume, Orange Flower. The woman in the picture had been Aunt Amy, but she was only a ghost in a frame, and a sad, pretty story from old times. She had been beautiful, much loved, unhappy, and she had died young.

Maria and Miranda, aged twelve and eight years, knew they were young, though they felt they had lived a long time. They had lived not only their own years; but their memories, it seemed to them, began years before they were born, in the lives of the grown-ups around them, old people above forty, most of them, who had a way of insisting that they too had been young once. It was hard to believe.

Their father was Aunt Amy's brother Harry. She had been his favorite sister. He sometimes glanced at the photograph and said, "It's not very good. Her hair and her smile were her chief beauties, and they aren't shown at all. She was much slimmer than that, too. There were never any fat women in the family, thank God."

When they heard their father say things like that, Maria and Miranda simply wondered, without criticism, what he meant. Their grandmother was thin as a match; the pictures of their mother, long since dead, proved her to have been a candle-wick, almost. Dashing young ladies, who turned out to be, to Miranda's astonishment, merely more of Grandmother's grandchildren, like herself, came visiting from school for the holidays, boasting of their eighteen-inch waists. But how did their father account for Great-aunt Eliza, who quite squeezed herself through doors, and who, when seated, was one solid pyramidal monument from floor to neck? What about Great-aunt Keziah, in Kentucky? Her husband, Great-uncle John Jacob, had refused to allow her to ride his good horses after she had achieved two hundred and twenty pounds. "No," said Great-uncle John Jacob, "my sentiments of chivalry are not dead in my bosom; but neither is my common sense, to say nothing of charity to our faithful dumb friends. And the greatest of these is charity." It was suggested to Great-uncle John Jacob that charity should forbid him to wound Great-aunt Keziah's female vanity by such a comment on her figure. "Female vanity will recover," said Great-uncle John Jacob, callously, "but what about my horses' backs? And if she had the proper female vanity in the first place, she would never have got into such shape." Well, Great-aunt Keziah was famous for her heft, and wasn't she in the family? But something seemed to happen to their father's memory when he thought of the girls he had known in the family of his youth, and he declared steadfastly they had all been, in every generation without exception, as slim as reeds and graceful as sylphs.

This loyalty of their father's in the face of evidence contrary to his ideal had its springs in family feeling, and a love of legend that he shared with the others. They loved to tell stories, romantic and poetic, or comic with a romantic humor; they did not gild the outward circumstance, it was the feeling that mattered. Their hearts and imaginations were captivated by their past, a past in which worldly considerations had played a very minor role. Their stories were almost always love stories against a bright blank heavenly blue sky.

Photographs, portraits by inept painters who meant earnestly to flatter, and the festival garments folded away in dried herbs and camphor were disappointing when the little girls tried to fit them to the living beings created in their minds by the breathing words of their elders. Grandmother, twice a year compelled in her blood by the change of seasons, would sit nearly all of one day beside old trunks and boxes in the lumber room, unfolding layers of garments and small keepsakes; she spread them out on sheets on the floor around her, crying over certain things, nearly always the same things, looking again at pictures in velvet cases, unwrapping locks of hair and dried flowers, crying gently and easily as if tears were the only pleasure she had left.

If Maria and Miranda were very quiet, and touched nothing until it was offered, they might sit by her at these times, or come and go. There was a tacit understanding that her grief was strictly her own, and must not be noticed or mentioned. The little girls examined the objects, one by one, and did not find them, in themselves, impressive. Such dowdy little wreaths and necklaces, some of them made of pearly shells; such moth-eaten bunches of pink ostrich feathers for the hair; such clumsy big breast pins and bracelets of gold and colored enamel; such silly-looking combs, standing up on tall teeth capped with seed pearls and French paste. Miranda, without knowing why, felt melancholy. It seemed such a pity that these faded things, these yellowed long gloves and misshapen satin slippers, these broad ribbons cracking where they were folded, should have been all those vanished girls had to decorate themselves with. And where were they now, those girls, and the boys in the odd-looking collars? The young men seemed even more unreal than the girls, with their high-buttoned coats, their puffy neckties, their waxed mustaches, their waving thick hair combed carefully over their foreheads. Who could have taken them seriously, looking like that?

No, Maria and Miranda found it impossible to sympathize with those young persons, sitting rather stiffly before the camera, hopelessly out of fashion; but they were drawn and held by the mysterious love of the living, who remembered and cherished these dead. The visible remains were nothing; they were dust, perishable as the flesh; the features stamped on paper and metal were nothing, but their living memory enchanted the little girls. They listened, all ears and eager minds, picking here and there among the floating ends of narrative, patching together as well as they could fragments of tales that were like bits of poetry or music, indeed were associated with the poetry they had heard or read, with music, with the theater.

"Tell me again how Aunt Amy went away when she was married." "She ran into the gray cold and stepped into the carriage and turned and smiled with her face as pale as death, and called out 'Good-by, good-by,' and refused her cloak, and said, 'Give me a glass of wine.' And none of us saw her alive again." "Why wouldn't she wear her cloak, Cousin Cora?" "Because she was not in love, my dear." Ruin hath taught me thus to ruminate, that time will come and take my love away. "Was she really beautiful, Uncle Bill?" "As an angel, my child." There were golden-haired angels with long blue pleated skirts dancing around the throne of the Blessed Virgin. None of them resembled Aunt Amy in the least, nor the type of beauty they had been brought up to admire. There were points of beauty by which one was judged severely. First, a beauty must be tall; whatever color the eyes, the hair must be dark, the darker the better; the skin must be pale and smooth. Lightness and swiftness of movement were important points. A beauty must be a good dancer, superb on horse-back, with a serene manner, an amiable gaiety tempered with dignity at all hours. Beautiful teeth and hands, of course, and over and above all this, some mysterious crown of enchantment that attracted and held the heart. It was all very exciting and discouraging.

Miranda persisted through her childhood in believing, in spite of her smallness, thinness, her little snubby nose saddled with freckles, her speckled gray eyes and habitual tantrums, that by some miracle she would grow into a tall, cream-colored brunette, like Cousin Isabel; she decided always to wear a trailing white satin gown. Maria, born sensible, had no such illusions. "We are going to take after Mamma's family," she said. "It's no use, we are. We'll never be beautiful, we'll always have freckles. And *you*," she told Miranda, "haven't even a good disposition."

Miranda admitted both truth and justice in this unkindness, but still secretly believed that she would one day suddenly receive beauty, as by inheritance, riches laid suddenly in her hands through no deserts of her own. She believed for quite a while that she would one day be like Aunt Amy, not as she appeared in the photograph, but as she was remembered by those who had seen her.

When Cousin Isabel came out in her tight black riding habit, surrounded by young men, and mounted gracefully, drawing her horse up and around so that he pranced learnedly on one spot while the other riders sprang to their saddles in the same sedate flurry, Miranda's heart would close with such a keen dart of admiration, envy, vicarious pride it was almost painful; but there would always be an elder present to lay a cooling hand upon her emotions. "She rides almost as well as Amy, doesn't she? But Amy had the pure Spanish style, she could bring out paces in a horse no one else knew he had." Young namesake Amy, on her way to a dance, would swish through the hall in ruffled white taffeta, glimmering like a moth in the lamplight, carrying her elbows pointed backward stiffly as wings, sliding along as if she were on rollers, in the fashionable walk of her day. She was considered the best dancer at any party, and Maria, sniffing the wave of perfume that followed Amy, would clasp her hands and say, "Oh, I can't *wait* to be grown up." But the elders would agree that the first Amy had been lighter, more smooth and delicate in her waltzing; young Amy would never equal her. Cousin Molly Parrington, far past her youth, indeed she belonged to the generation before Aunt Amy, was a noted charmer. Men who had known her all her life still gathered about her; now that she was happily widowed for the second time there was no doubt that she would yet marry again. But Amy, said the elders, had the same high spirits and wit without boldness, and you really could not say that Molly had ever been discreet. She dyed her hair, and made jokes about it. She had a way of collecting the men around her in a corner, where she told them stories. She was an unnatural mother to her ugly daughter Eva, an old maid past forty while her mother was still the belle of the ball. "Born when I was fifteen, you remember," Molly would say shamelessly, looking an old beau straight in the eye, both of them remembering that he had been best man at her first wedding when she was past twenty-one. "Everyone said I was like a little girl with her doll."

Eva, shy and chinless, straining her upper lip over two enormous teeth, would sit in corners watching her mother. She looked hungry, her eyes were strained and tired. She wore her mother's old clothes, made over, and taught Latin in a Female Seminary. She believed in votes for women, and had traveled about, making speeches. When her mother was not present, Eva bloomed out a little, danced prettily, smiled, showing all her teeth, and was like a dry little plant set out in a gentle rain. Molly was merry about her ugly duckling. "It's lucky for me my daughter is an old maid. She's not so apt," said Molly naughtily, "to make a grandmother of me." Eva would blush as if she had been slapped.

Eva was a blot, no doubt about it, but the little girls felt she belonged to their everyday world of dull lessons to be learned, stiff shoes to be limbered up, scratchy flannels to be endured in cold weather, measles and disappointed expectations. Their Aunt Amy belonged to the world of poetry. The romance of Uncle Gabriel's long, unrewarded love for her, her early death, was such a story as one found in old books: unworldly books, but true, such as the Vita Nuova, the Sonnets of Shakespeare and the Wedding Song of Spenser; and poems by Edgar Allan Poe. "Her tantalized spirit now blandly reposes, Forgetting or never regretting its roses. . . ." Their father read that to them, and said, "He was our greatest poet," and they knew that "our" meant he was Southern. Aunt Amy was real as the pictures in the old Holbein and Dürer books were real. The little girls lay flat on their stomachs and peered into a world of wonder, turning the shabby leaves that fell apart easily, not surprised at the sight of the Mother of God sitting on a hollow log nursing her Child; not doubting either Death or the Devil riding at the stirrups of the grim knight; not questioning the propriety of the stiffly dressed ladies of Sir Thomas More's household, seated in dignity on the floor, or seeming to be. They missed all the dog and pony shows, and lantern-slide entertainments, but their father took them to see "Hamlet," and "The Taming of the Shrew," and "Richard the Third," and a long

115

sad play with Mary, Queen of Scots, in it. Miranda
thought the magnificent lady in black velvet was
truly the Queen of Scots, and was pained to learn
that the real Queen had died long ago, and not at all
on the night she, Miranda, had been present.

The little girls loved the theater, that world of
personages taller than human beings, who swept upon
the scene and invested it with their presences, their
more than human voices, their gestures of gods and
goddesses ruling a universe. But there was always
a voice recalling other and greater occasions. Grandmother in her youth had heard Jenny Lind, and
thought that Nellie Melba was much overrated.
Father had seen Bernhardt, and Madame Modjeska
was no sort of rival. When Paderewski played for
the first time in their city, cousins came from all over
the state and went from the Grandmother's house to
hear him. The little girls were left out of this great
occasion. They shared the excitement of the going
away, and shared the beautiful moment of return,
when cousins stood about in groups, with coffee cups
and glasses in their hands, talking in low voices,
awed and happy. The little girls, struck with the
sense of a great event, hung about in their night-
gowns and listened, until someone noticed and hustled
them away from the sweet nimbus of all that glory.
One old gentleman, however, had heard Rubinstein
frequently. He could not but feel that Rubinstein
had reached the final height of musical interpreta-
tion, and, for him, Paderewski had been something of
an anticlimax. The little girls heard him muttering
on, holding up one hand, patting the air as if he

were calling for silence. The others looked at him, and listened, without any disturbance of their grave tender mood. They had never heard Rubinstein; they had, one hour since, heard Paderewski, and why should anyone need to recall the past? Miranda, dragged away, half understanding the old gentleman, hated him. She felt that she too had heard Paderewski.

There was then a life beyond a life in this world, as well as in the next; such episodes confirmed for the little girls the nobility of human feeling, the divinity of man's vision of the unseen, the importance of life and death, the depths of the human heart, the romantic value of tragedy. Cousin Eva, on a certain visit, trying to interest them in the study of Latin, told them the story of John Wilkes Booth, who, handsomely garbed in a long black cloak, had leaped to the stage after assassinating President Lincoln. "Sic semper tyrannis," he had shouted superbly, in spite of his broken leg. The little girls never doubted that it had happened in just that way, and the moral seemed to be that one should always have Latin, or at least a good classical poetry quotation, to depend upon in great or desperate moments. Cousin Eva reminded them that no one, not even a good Southerner, could possibly approve of John Wilkes Booth's deed. It was murder, after all. They were to remember that. But Miranda, used to tragedy in books and in family legends—two great-uncles had committed suicide and a remote ancestress had gone mad for love—decided that, without the murder, there would have been no point to dressing u and leaping to the stage shouting in Latin. So how could she disapprove of the deed? It was a fine story. She knew a distantly related old gentleman who had been devoted to the art of Booth, had seen him in a great many plays, but not, alas, at his greatest moment. Miranda regretted this; it would have been so pleasant to have the assassination of Lincoln in the family.

Uncle Gabriel, who had loved Aunt Amy so desperately, still lived somewhere, though Miranda and Maria had never seen him. He had gone away, far away, after her death. He still owned racehorses, and ran them at famous tracks all over the country, and Miranda believed there could not possibly be a more brilliant career. He had married again, quite soon, and had written to Grandmother, asking her to accept his new wife as a daughter in place of Amy. Grandmother had written coldly, accepting, inviting them for a visit, but Uncle Gabriel had somehow never brought his bride home. Harry had visited them in New Orleans, and reported that the second wife was a very good-looking well-bred blonde girl who would undoubtedly be a good wife for Gabriel. Still, Uncle Gabriel's heart was broken. Faithfully once a year he wrote a letter to someone of the family, sending money for a wreath for Amy's grave. He had written a poem for her gravestone, and had come home, leaving his second wife in Atlanta, to see that it was carved properly. He could never account for having written this poem; he had certainly never tried to write a single rhyme since leaving school. Yet one day when he had been thinking about Amy, the verse occurred to him, out of the air. Maria and Miranda had seen it, printed in gold on a mourning card. Uncle Gabriel had sent a great number of them to be handed around among the family.

> "She lives again who suffered life,
>   Then suffered death, and now set free
>   A singing angel, she forgets
>   The griefs of old mortality."

"Did she really sing?" Maria asked her father.

"Now what has that to do with it?" he asked. "It's a poem."

"I think it's very pretty," said Miranda, impressed. Uncle Gabriel was second cousin to her father and Aunt Amy. It brought poetry very near.

"Not so bad for tombstone poetry," said their father, "but it should be better."

Uncle Gabriel had waited five years to marry Aunt Amy. She had been ill, her chest was weak; she was engaged twice to other young men and broke her engagements for no reason; and she laughed at the advice of older and kinder-hearted persons who thought it very capricious of her not to return the devotion of such a handsome and romantic young man as Gabriel, her second cousin, too; it was not as if she would be marrying a stranger. Her coldness was said to have driven Gabriel to a wild life and even to drinking. His grandfather was wealthy and Gabriel was his favorite; they had quarreled over the racehorses, and Gabriel had shouted, "By God, I must have *something*." As if he had not everything already: youth, health, good looks, the prospect of riches, and a devoted family circle. His grandfather pointed out to him that he was little better than an ingrate, and showed signs of being a wastrel as well. Gabriel said, "You had racehorses, and made a good thing of them." "I never depended upon them for a livelihood, sir," said his grandfather.

Gabriel wrote letters about this and many other things to Amy from Saratoga and from Kentucky and from New Orleans, sending her presents, and flowers packed in ice, and telegrams. The presents were amusing, such as a huge cage full of small green lovebirds; or, as an ornament for her hair, a full-petaled enameled rose with paste dewdrops, with an enameled butterfly in brilliant colors suspended quivering on a gold wire about it; but the telegrams always frightened her mother, and the flowers, after a journey by train and then by stage into the country, were much the worse for wear. He would send roses when the rose garden at home was in full bloom. Amy could not help smiling over it, though her mother insisted it was touching and sweet of Gabriel. It must prove to Amy that she was always in his thoughts.

"That's no place for me," said Amy, but she had a way of speaking, a tone of voice, which made it impossible to discover what she meant by what she said. It was possible always that she might be serious. And she would not answer questions.

"Amy's wedding dress," said the Grandmother, unfurling an immense cloak of dove-colored cut velvet, spreading beside it a silvery-gray watered-silk frock, and a small gray velvet toque with a dark red breast of feathers. Cousin Isabel, the beauty, sat with her. They talked to each other, and Miranda could listen if she chose.

"She would not wear white, nor a veil," said Grandmother. "I couldn't oppose her, for I had said my daughters should each have exactly the wedding dress they wanted. But Amy surprised me. 'Now what would I look like in white satin?' she asked. It's true she was pale, but she would have been angelic in it, and all of us told her so. 'I shall wear mourning if I like,' she said, 'it is *my* funeral, you know.' I reminded her that Lou and your mother had worn white with veils and it would please me to have my daughters all alike in that. Amy said, 'Lou and Isabel are not like me,' but I could not persuade her to explain what she meant. One day when she was ill she said, 'Mammy, I'm not long for this world,' but not as if she meant it. I told her, 'You might live as long as anyone, if only you will be sensible.' 'That's the whole trouble,' said Amy. 'I feel sorry for Gabriel,' she told me. 'He doesn't know what he's asking for.'

"I tried to tell her once more," said the Grandmother, "that marriage and children would cure her of everything. 'All women of our family are delicate when they are young,' I said. 'Why, when I was your age no one expected me to live a year. It was called greensickness, and everybody knew there was only one cure.' 'If I live for a hundred years and turn green as grass,' said Amy, 'I still shan't want to marry Gabriel.' So I told her very seriously that if she truly felt that way she must never do it, and Gabriel must be told once for all, and sent away. He would get over it. 'I have told him, and I have sent him away,' said Amy. 'He just doesn't listen.' We both laughed at that, and I told her young girls found a hundred ways to deny they wished to be married, and a thousand more to test their power over men, but that she had more than enough of that, and now it was time for her to be entirely sincere and make her decision. As for me," said the Grandmother, "I wished with all heart to marry your grandfather, and if he had not asked me, I should have asked him most certainly. Amy insisted that she could not imagine wanting to marry anybody. She would be, she said, a nice old maid like Eva Parrington. For even then it was pretty plain that Eva was an old maid, born. Harry said, 'Oh, Eva—Eva has no chin, that's her trouble. If you had no chin, Amy, you'd be in the same fix as Eva, no doubt.' Your Uncle Bill would say, 'When women haven't anything else, they'll take a vote for consolation. A pretty thin bed-fellow,' said your Uncle Bill. 'What I really need is a good dancing partner to guide me through life,' said Amy, 'that's the match I'm looking for.' It was no good trying to talk to her."

Her brothers remembered her tenderly as a sensible girl. After listening to their comments on her character and ways, Maria decided that they considered her sensible because she asked their advice about her appearance when she was going out to dance. If they found fault in any way, she would change her dress or her hair until they were pleased, and say, "You are an angel not to let your poor sister go out looking like a freak." But she would not listen to her father, nor to Gabriel. If Gabriel praised the frock she was wearing, she was apt to disappear and come back in another. He loved her long black hair, and once, lifting it up from her pillow when she was ill, said, "I love your hair, Amy, the most beautiful hair in the world." When he returned on his next visit, he found her with her hair cropped and curled close to her head. He was horrified, as if she had willfully mutilated herself. She would not let it grow again, not even to please her brothers. The photograph hanging on the wall was one she had made at that time to send to Gabriel, who sent it back without a word. This pleased her, and she framed the photograph. There was a thin inky scrawl low in one corner, "To dear brother Harry, who likes my hair cut."

This was a mischievous reference to a very grave scandal. The little girls used to look at their father, and wonder what would have happened if he had really hit the young man he shot at. The young man was believed to have kissed Aunt Amy, when she was not in the least engaged to him. Uncle Gabriel was supposed to have had a duel with the young man, but Father had got there first. He was a pleasant, everyday sort of father, who held his daughters on his knee if they were prettily dressed and well behaved, and pushed them away if they had not freshly combed hair and nicely scrubbed fingernails. "Go away, you're disgusting," he would say, in a matter-of-fact voice. He noticed if their stocking seams were crooked. He caused them to brush their teeth with a revolting mixture of prepared chalk, powdered charcoal, and salt. When they behaved stupidly he could not endure the sight of them. They understood dimly that all this was for their own future good; and when they were snivelly with colds, he prescribed delicious hot toddy for them, and saw that it was given them. He was always hoping they might not grow up to be so silly as they seemed to him at any given moment, and he had a disconcerting way of inquiring, "How do you *know?*" when they forgot and made dogmatic statements in his presence. It always came out embarrassingly that they did not know at all, but were repeating something they had heard. This made conversation with him difficult, for he laid traps and they fell into them, but it became important to them that their father should not believe them to be fools. Well, this very father had gone to Mexico once and stayed there for nearly a year, because he had shot at a man with whom Aunt Amy had flirted at a dance. It had been very wrong of him, because he should have challenged the man to a duel, as Uncle Gabriel had done. Instead, he just took a shot at him, and this was the lowest sort of manners. It had caused great disturbance in the whole community and had almost broken up the affair between Aunt Amy and Uncle Gabriel for good. Uncle Gabriel insisted that the young man had kissed Aunt Amy, and Aunt Amy insisted that the young man had merely paid her a compliment on her hair.

During the Mardi Gras holidays there was to be a big gay fancy-dress ball. Harry was going as a bull-fighter because his sweetheart, Mariana, had a new black lace mantilla and high comb from Mexico. Maria and Miranda had seen a photograph of their mother in this dress, her lovely face without a trace of coquetry looking gravely out from under a tremendous fall of lace from the peak of the comb, a rose tucked firmly over her ear. Amy copied her costume from a small Dresden-china shepherdess which stood on the mantelpiece in the parlor; a careful copy with ribboned hat, gilded crook, very low-laced bodice, short basket skirts, green slippers and all. She wore it with a black half-mask, but it was no disguise. "You would have known it was Amy at any distance," said Father. Gabriel, six feet three in height as he was, had got himself up to match, and a spectacle he provided in pale blue satin knee breeches and a blond curled wig with a hair ribbon. "He felt a fool, and he looked like one," said Uncle Bill, "and he behaved like one before the evening was over."

Everything went beautifully until the party gathered downstairs to leave for the ball. Amy's father —he must have been born a grandfather, thought Miranda—gave one glance at his daughter, her white ankles shining, bosom deeply exposed, two round spots of paint on her cheeks, and fell into a frenzy of outraged propriety. "It's disgraceful," he pronounced, loudly. "No daughter of mine is going to show herself in such a rig-out. It's bawdy," he thundered. "Bawdy!"

Amy had taken off her mask to smile at him. "Why, Papa," she said very sweetly, "what's wrong with it? Look on the mantelpiece. She's been there all along, and you were never shocked before."

"There's all the difference in the world," said her father, "all the difference, young lady, and you know it. You go upstairs this minute and pin up that waist in front and let down those skirts to a decent length before you leave this house. *And wash your face!*"

"I see nothing wrong with it," said Amy's mother, firmly, "and you shouldn't use such language before innocent young girls." She and Amy sat down with several females of the household to help, and they made short work of the business. In ten minutes Amy returned, face clean, bodice filled in with lace, shepherdess skirt modestly sweeping the carpet behind her.

When Amy appeared from the dressing room for her first dance with Gabriel, the lace was gone from her bodice, her skirts were tucked up more daringly than before, and the spots on her cheeks were like pomegranates. "Now Gabriel, tell me truly, wouldn't it have been a pity to spoil my costume?" Gabriel, delighted that she had asked his opinion, declared it was perfect. They agreed with kindly tolerance that old people were often tiresome, but one need not upset them by open disobedience: their youth was gone, what had they to live for?

Harry, dancing with Mariana who swung a heavy train around her expertly at every turn of the waltz, began to be uneasy about his sister Amy. She was entirely too popular. He saw young men make beelines across the floor, eyes fixed on those white silk ankles. Some of the young men he did not know at all, others he knew too well and could not approve of for his sister Amy. Gabriel, unhappy in his lyric satin and wig, stood about holding his ribboned crook as though it had sprouted thorns. He hardly danced at all with Amy, he did not enjoy dancing with anyone else, and he was having a thoroughly wretched time of it.

There appeared late, alone, got up as Jean Lafitte, a young Creole gentleman who had, two years before, been for a time engaged to Amy. He came straight to her, with the manner of a happy lover, and said, clearly enough for everyone near by to hear him, "I only came because I knew you were to be here. I only want to dance with you and I shall go again." Amy, with a face of delight, cried out, "Raymond!" as if to a lover. She had danced with him four times, and had then disappeared from the floor on his arm.

Harry and Mariana, in conventional disguise of romance, irreproachably betrothed, safe in their happiness, were waltzing slowly to their favorite song, the melancholy farewell of the Moorish King on leaving Granada. They sang in whispers to each other, in their uncertain Spanish, a song of love and parting and that sword's point of grief that makes the heart tender toward all other lost and disinherited creatures: Oh, mansion of love, my earthly paradise . . . that I shall see no more . . . whither flies the poor swallow, weary and homeless, seeking for shelter where no shelter is? I too am far from

home without the power to fly. . . . Come to my
heart, sweet bird, beloved pilgrim, build your nest
near my bed, let me listen to your song, and weep
for my lost land of joy. . . .

Into this bliss broke Gabriel. He had thrown away
his shepherd's crook and he was carrying his wig.
He wanted to speak to Harry at once, and before
Mariana knew what was happening she was sitting
beside her mother and the two excited young men
were gone. Waiting, disturbed and displeased, she
smiled at Amy who waltzed past with a young man
in Devil costume, including ill-fitting scarlet cloven
hoofs. Almost at once, Harry and Gabriel came back,
with serious faces, and Harry darted on the dance
floor, returning with Amy. The girls and the chaper-
ones were asked to come at once, they must be taken
home. It was all mysterious and sudden, and Harry
said to Mariana, "I will tell you what is happening,
but not now—"

The Grandmother remembered of this disgraceful
affair only that Gabriel brought Amy home alone
and that Harry came in somewhat later. The other
members of the party straggled in at various hours,
and the story came out piecemeal. Amy was silent
and, her mother discovered later, burning with fever.
"I saw at once that something was very wrong.
'What has happened, Amy?' 'Oh, Harry goes about
shooting at people at a party,' she said, sitting down
as if she were exhausted. 'It was on your account,
Amy,' said Gabriel. 'Oh, no, it was not,' said Amy.
'Don't believe him, Mammy.' So I said, 'Now enough
of this. Tell me what happened, Amy.' And Amy

said, 'Mammy, this is it. Raymond came in, and you know I like Raymond, and he is a good dancer. So we danced together, too much, maybe. We went on the gallery for a breath of air, and stood there. He said, "How well your hair looks. I like this new shingled style." ' She glanced at Gabriel. 'And then another young man came out and said, "I've been looking everywhere. This is our dance, isn't it?" And I went in to dance. And now it seems that Gabriel went out at once and challenged Raymond to a duel about something or other, but Harry doesn't wait for that. Raymond had already gone out to have his horse brought, I suppose one doesn't duel in fancy dress,' she said, looking at Gabriel, who fairly shriveled in his blue satin shepherd's costume, 'and Harry simply went out and shot at him. I don't think that was fair,' said Amy."

Her mother agreed that indeed it was not fair; it was not even decent, and she could not imagine what her son Harry thought he was doing. "It isn't much of a way to defend your sister's honor," she said to him afterward. "I didn't want Gabriel to go fighting duels," said Harry. "That wouldn't have helped much, either."

Gabriel had stood before Amy, leaning over, asking once more the question he had apparently been asking her all the way home. "Did he kiss you, Amy?"

Amy took off her shepherdess hat and pushed her hair back. "Maybe he did," she answered, "and maybe I wished him to."

"Amy, you must not say such things," said her mother. "Answer Gabriel's question."

"He hasn't the right to ask it," said Amy, but without anger.

"Do you love him, Amy?" asked Gabriel, the sweat standing out on his forehead.

"It doesn't matter," answered Amy, leaning back in her chair.

"Oh, it does matter; it matters terribly," said Gabriel. "You must answer me now." He took both of her hands and tried to hold them. She drew her hands away firmly and steadily so that he had to let go.

"Let her alone, Gabriel," said Amy's mother. "You'd better go now. We are all tired. Let's talk about it tomorrow."

She helped Amy to undress, noticing the changed bodice and the shortened skirt. "You shouldn't have done that, Amy. That was not wise of you. It was better the other way."

Amy said, "Mammy, I'm sick of this world. I don't like anything in it. It's so *dull*," she said, and for a moment she looked as if she might weep. She had never been tearful, even as a child, and her mother was alarmed. It was then she discovered that Amy had fever.

"Gabriel is dull, Mother—he sulks," she said. "I could see him sulking every time I passed. It spoils things," she said. "Oh, I want to go to sleep."

Her mother sat looking at her and wondering how it had happened she had brought such a beautiful child into the world. "Her face," said her mother, "was angelic in sleep."

Some time during that fevered night, the projected duel between Gabriel and Raymond was halted by the offices of friends on both sides. There remained the open question of Harry's impulsive shot, which was not so easily settled. Raymond seemed vindictive about that, it was possible he might choose to make trouble. Harry, taking the advice of Gabriel, his brothers and friends, decided that the best way to avoid further scandal was for him to disappear for a while. This being decided upon, the young men returned about daybreak, saddled Harry's best horse and helped him pack a few things; accompanied by Gabriel and Bill, Harry set out for the border, feeling rather gay and adventurous.

Amy, being wakened by the stirring in the house, found out the plan. Five minutes after they were gone, she came down in her riding dress, had her own horse saddled, and struck out after them. She rode almost every morning; before her parents had time to be uneasy over her prolonged absence, they found her note.

What had threatened to be a tragedy became a rowdy lark. Amy rode to the border, kissed her brother Harry good-by, and rode back again with Bill and Gabriel. It was a three days' journey, and when they arrived Amy had to be lifted from the saddle. She was really ill by now, but in the gayest of humors. Her mother and father had been prepared to be severe with her, but, at sight of her, their feelings changed. They turned on Bill and Gabriel. "Why did you let her do this?" they asked.

"You know we could not stop her," said Gabriel helplessly, "and she did enjoy herself so much!"

Amy laughed. "Mammy, it was splendid, the most delightful trip I ever had. And if I am to be the heroine of this novel, why shouldn't I make the most of it?"

The scandal, Maria and Miranda gathered, had been pretty terrible. Amy simply took to bed and stayed there, and Harry had skipped out blithely to wait until the little affair blew over. The rest of the family had to receive visitors, write letters, go to church, return calls, and bear the whole brunt, as they expressed it. They sat in the twilight of scandal in their little world, holding themselves very rigidly, in a shared tension as if all their nerves began at a common center. This center had received a blow, and family nerves shuddered, even into the farthest reaches of Kentucky. From whence in due time Great-great-aunt Sally Rhea addressed a letter to *Mifs Amy Rhea*. In deep brown ink like dried blood, in a spidery hand adept at archaic symbols and abbreviations, Great-great-aunt Sally informed Amy that she was fairly convinced that this calamity was only the forerunner of a series shortly to be visited by the Almighty God upon a race already condemned through its own wickedness, a warning that man's time was short, and that they must all prepare for the end of the world. For herself, she had long expected it, she was entirely resigned to the prospect of meeting her Maker; and Amy, no less than her wicked brother Harry, must likewise place herself in God's hands and prepare for the worst. *"Oh, my dear unfortunate young relative,"* twittered Great-great-aunt Sally, *"we must in our Extremty join hands and appr before ye Dread Throne of Jdgmnt a United Fmly, if One is Mssg from ye Flock, what will Jesus say?"*

Great-great-aunt Sally's religious career had become comic legend. She had forsaken her Catholic rearing for a young man whose family were Cumberland Presbyterians. Unable to accept their opinions, however, she was converted to the Hard-Shell Baptists, a sect as loathsome to her husband's family as the Catholic could possibly be. She had spent a life of vicious self-indulgent martyrdom to her faith; as Harry commented: "Religion put claws on Aunt Sally and gave her a post to whet them on." She had out-argued, out-fought, and out-lived her entire generation, but she did not miss them. She bedeviled the second generation without ceasing, and was beginning hungrily on the third.

Amy, reading this letter, broke into her gay full laugh that always caused everyone around her to laugh too, even before they knew why, and her small green lovebirds in their cage turned and eyed her solemnly. "Imagine drawing a pew in Heaven beside Aunt Sally," she said. "What a prospect."

"Don't laugh too soon," said her father. "Heaven was made to order for Aunt Sally. She'll be on her own territory there."

"For my sins," said Amy, "I must go to Heaven with Aunt Sally."

During the uncomfortable time of Harry's absence, Amy went on refusing to marry Gabriel. Her mother could hear their voices going on in their endless colloquy, during many long days. One afternoon Gabriel came out, looking very sober and discouraged. He stood looking down at Amy's mother as she sat sewing, and said, "I think it is all over, I believe now that Amy will never have me." The Grandmother always said afterward, "Never have I pitied anyone as I did poor Gabriel at that moment. But I told him, very firmly, 'Let her alone, then, she is ill.'" So Gabriel left, and Amy had no word from him for more than a month.

The day after Gabriel was gone, Amy rose looking extremely well, went hunting with her brothers Bill and Stephen, bought a velvet wrap, had her hair shingled and curled again, and wrote long letters to Harry, who was having a most enjoyable exile in Mexico City.

After dancing all night three times in one week, she woke one morning in a hemorrhage. She seemed frightened and asked for the doctor, promising to do whatever he advised. She was quiet for a few days, reading. She asked for Gabriel. No one knew where he was. "You should write him a letter; his mother will send it on." "Oh, no," she said. "I miss him coming in with his sour face. Letters are no good."

Gabriel did come in, only a few days later, with a very sour face and unpleasant news. His grandfather had died, after a day's illness. On his death bed, in the name of God, being of a sound and disposing mind, he had cut off his favorite grandchild Gabriel with one dollar. "In the name of God, Amy," said Gabriel, "the old devil has ruined me in one sentence."

It was the conduct of his immediate family in the matter that had embittered him, he said. They could hardly conceal their satisfaction. They had known and envied Gabriel's quite just, well-founded expectations. Not one of them offered to make any private settlement. No one even thought of repairing this last-minute act of senile vengeance. Privately they blessed their luck. "I have been cut off with a dollar," said Gabriel, "and they are all glad of it. I think they feel somehow that this justifies every criticism they ever made against me. They were right about me all along. I am a worthless poor relation," said Gabriel. "My God, I wish you could see them."

Amy said, "I wonder how you will ever support a wife, now."

Gabriel said, "Oh, it isn't so bad as that. If you would, Amy—"

Amy said. "Gabriel, if we get married now there'll be just time to be in New Orleans for Mardi Gras. If we wait until after Lent, it may be too late."

"Why, Amy," said Gabriel, "how could it ever be too late?"

"You might change your mind," said Amy. "You know how fickle you are."

There were two letters in the Grandmother's many packets of letters that Maria and Miranda read after they were grown. One of them was from Amy. It was dated ten days after her marriage.

"Dear Mammy, New Orleans hasn't changed as much as I have since we saw each other last. I am now a staid old married woman, and Gabriel is very devoted and kind. Footlights won a race for us yesterday, she was the favorite, and it was wonderful. I go to the races every day, and our horses are doing splendidly; I had my choice of Erin Go Bragh or Miss Lucy, and I chose Miss Lucy. She is mine now, she runs like a streak. Gabriel says I made a mistake, Erin Go Bragh will stay better. I think Miss Lucy will stay my time.

"We are having a lovely visit. I'm going to put on a domino and take to the streets with Gabriel sometime during Mardi Gras. I'm tired of watching the show from a balcony. Gabriel says it isn't safe. He says he'll take me if I insist, but I doubt it. Mammy, he's very nice. Don't worry about me. I have a beautiful black-and-rose-colored velvet gown for the Proteus Ball. Madame, my new mother-in-law, wanted to know if it wasn't a little dashing. I told her I hoped so or I had been cheated. It is fitted perfectly smooth in the bodice, very low in the shoulders—Papa would not approve—and the skirt is looped with wide silver ribbons between the waist and knees in front, and then it surges around and is looped enormously in the back, with a train just one yard long. I now have an eighteen-inch waist, thanks to Madame Duré. I expect to be so dashing that my mother-in-law will have an attack. She has them quite often. Gabriel sends love. Please take good care of Graylie and

Fiddler. I want to ride them again when I come home. We're going to Saratoga, I don't know just when. Give everybody my dear dear love. It rains all the time here, of course. . . .

"P.S. Mammy, as soon as I get a minute to myself, I'm going to be terribly homesick. Good-by, my darling Mammy."

The other was from Amy's nurse, dated six weeks after Amy's marriage.

"I cut off the lock of hair because I was sure you would like to have it. And I do not want you to think I was careless, leaving her medicine where she could get it, the doctor has written and explained. It would not have done her any harm except that her heart was weak. She did not know how much she was taking, often she said to me, one more of those little capsules wouldn't do any harm, and so I told her to be careful and not take anything except what I gave her. She begged me for them sometimes but I would not give her more than the doctor said. I slept during the night because she did not seem to be so sick as all that and the doctor did not order me to sit up with her. Please accept my regrets for your great loss and please do not think that anybody was careless with your dear daughter. She suffered a great deal and now she is at rest. She could not get well but she might have lived longer. Yours respectfully. . . ."

The letters and all the strange keepsakes were packed away and forgotten for a great many years. They seemed to have no place in the world.

Part II: 1904

Dᴜʀɪɴɢ vacation on their grandmother's farm, Maria and Miranda, who read as naturally and constantly as ponies crop grass, and with much the same kind of pleasure, had by some happy chance laid hold of some forbidden reading matter, brought in and left there with missionary intent, no doubt, by some Protestant cousin. It fell into the right hands if enjoyment had been its end. The reading matter was printed in poor type on spongy paper, and was ornamented with smudgy illustrations all the more exciting to the little girls because they could not make head or tail of them. The stories were about beautiful but unlucky maidens, who for mysterious reasons had been trapped by nuns and priests in dire collusion; they were then "immured" in convents, where they were forced to take the veil— an appalling rite during which the victims shrieked dreadfully—and condemned forever after to most uncomfortable and disorderly existences. They seemed to divide their time between lying chained in dark cells and assisting other nuns to bury throttled infants under stones in moldering rat-infested dungeons.

Immured! It was the word Maria and Miranda had been needing all along to describe their condition at the Convent of the Child Jesus, in New Orleans, where they spent the long winters trying to avoid an education. There were no dungeons at the Child Jesus, and this was only one of numerous marked differences between convent life as Maria and Miranda knew it and the thrilling paper-backed version. It was no good at all trying to fit the stories to life, and they did not even try. They had long since learned to draw the lines between life, which was real and earnest, and the grave was not its goal; poetry, which was true but not real; and stories, or forbidden reading matter, in which things happened as nowhere else, with the most sublime irrelevance and unlikelihood, and one need not turn a hair, because there was not a word of truth in them.

It was true the little girls were hedged and confined, but in a large garden with trees and a grotto; they were locked at night into a long cold dormitory, with all the windows open, and a sister sleeping at either end. Their beds were curtained with muslin, and small night-lamps were so arranged that the sisters could see through the curtains, but the children could not see the sisters. Miranda wondered if they ever slept, or did they sit there all night quietly watching the sleepers through the muslin? She tried to work up a little sinister thrill about this, but she found it impossible to care much what either of the sisters did. They were very dull good-natured women who managed to make the whole dormitory seem dull. All days and all things in the Convent of the Child

Jesus were dull, in fact, and Maria and Miranda lived for Saturdays.

No one had even hinted that they should become nuns. On the contrary Miranda felt that the discouraging attitude of Sister Claude and Sister Austin and Sister Ursula toward her expressed ambition to be a nun barely veiled a deeply critical knowledge of her spiritual deficiencies. Still Maria and Miranda had got a fine new word out of their summer reading, and they referred to themselves as "immured." It gave a romantic glint to what was otherwise a very dull life for them, except for blessed Saturday afternoons during the racing season.

If the nuns were able to assure the family that the deportment and scholastic achievements of Maria and Miranda were at least passable, some cousin or other always showed up smiling, in holiday mood, to take them to the races, where they were given a dollar each to bet on any horse they chose. There were black Saturdays now and then, when Maria and Miranda sat ready, hats in hand, curly hair plastered down and slicked behind their ears, their stiffly pleated navy-blue skirts spread out around them, waiting with their hearts going down slowly into their high-topped laced-up black shoes. They never put on their hats until the last minute, for somehow it would have been too horrible to have their hats on, when, after all, Cousin Henry and Cousin Isabel, or Uncle George and Aunt Polly, were not coming to take them to the races. When no one appeared, and Saturday came and went a sickening waste, they were then given to understand that it was a punishment for bad marks during the week. They never knew until it was too late to avoid the disappointment. It was very wearing.

One Saturday they were sent down to wait in the visitors' parlor, and there was their father. He had come all the way from Texas to see them. They leaped at sight of him, and then stopped short, suspiciously. Was he going to take them to the races? If so, they were happy to see him.

"Hello," said Father, kissing their cheeks. "Have you been good girls? Your Uncle Gabriel is running a mare at the Crescent City today, so we'll all go and bet on her. Would you like that?"

Maria put on her hat without a word, but Miranda stood and addressed her father sternly. She had suffered many doubts about this day. "*Why* didn't you send word yesterday? I could have been looking forward all this time."

"We didn't know," said Father, in his easiest paternal manner, "that you were going to deserve it. Remember Saturday before last?"

Miranda hung her head and put on her hat, with the round elastic under the chin. She remembered too well. She had, in midweek, given way to despair over her arithmetic and had fallen flat on her face on the classroom floor, refusing to rise until she was carried out. The rest of the week had been a series of novel deprivations, and Saturday a day of mourning; secret mourning, for if one mourned too noisily, it simply meant another bad mark against deportment.

"Never mind," said Father, as if it were the

smallest possible matter, "today you're going. Come along now. We've barely time."

These expeditions were all joy, every time, from the moment they stepped into a closed one-horse cab, a treat in itself with its dark, thick upholstery, soaked with strange perfumes and tobacco smoke, until the thrilling moment when they walked into a restaurant under big lights and were given dinner with things to eat they never had at home, much less at the convent. They felt worldly and grown up, each with her glass of water colored pink with claret.

The great crowd was always exciting as if they had never seen it before, with the beautiful, incredibly dressed ladies, all plumes and flowers and paint, and the elegant gentlemen with yellow gloves. The bands played in turn with thundering drums and brasses, and now and then a wild beautiful horse would career around the track with a tiny, monkey-shaped boy on his back, limbering up for his race.

Miranda had a secret personal interest in all this which she knew better than to confide to anyone, even Maria. Least of all to Maria. In ten minutes the whole family would have known. She had lately decided to be a jockey when she grew up. Her father had said one day that she was going to be a little thing all her life, she would never be tall; and this meant, of course, that she would never be a beauty like Aunt Amy, or Cousin Isabel. Her hope of being a beauty died hard, until the notion of being a jockey came suddenly and filled all her thoughts. Quietly, blissfully, at night before she slept, and too often in the daytime when she should have been studying, she planned her career as jockey. It was dim in detail, but brilliant at the right distance. It seemed too silly to be worried about arithmetic at all, when what she needed for her future was to ride better—much better. "You ought to be ashamed of yourself," said Father, after watching her gallop full tilt down the lane at the farm, on Trixie, the mustang mare. "I can see the sun, moon and stars between you and the saddle every jump." Spanish style meant that one sat close to the saddle, and did all kinds of things with the knees and reins. Jockeys bounced lightly, their knees almost level with the horse's back, rising and falling like a rubber ball. Miranda felt she could do that easily. Yes, she would be a jockey, like Tod Sloan, winning every other race at least. Meantime, while she was training, she would keep it a secret, and one day she would ride out, bouncing lightly, with the other jockeys, and win a great race, and surprise everybody, her family most of all.

On that particular Saturday, her idol, the great Tod Sloan, was riding, and he won two races. Miranda longed to bet her dollar on Tod Sloan, but father said, "Not now, honey. Today you must bet on Uncle Gabriel's horse. Save your dollar for the fourth race, and put it on Miss Lucy. You've got a hundred to one shot. Think if she wins."

Miranda knew well enough that a hundred to one shot was no bet at all. She sulked, the crumpled dollar in her hand grew damp and warm. She could have won three dollars already on Tod Sloan. Maria said virtuously, "It wouldn't be nice not to bet on Uncle Gabriel. That way, we keep the money in the family." Miranda put out her under lip at her sister. Maria was too prissy for words. She wrinkled her nose back at Miranda.

They had just turned their dollar over to the bookmaker for the fourth race when a vast bulging man with a red face and immense tan ragged mustaches fading into gray hailed them from a lower level of the grandstand, over the heads of the crowd, "Hey, there, Harry?" Father said, "Bless my soul, there's Gabriel." He motioned to the man, who came pushing his way heavily up the shallow steps. Maria and Miranda stared, first at him, then at each other. "Can that be our Uncle Gabriel?" their eyes asked. "Is that Aunt Amy's handsome romantic beau? Is that the man who wrote the poem about our Aunt Amy?" Oh, what did grown-up people *mean* when they talked, anyway?

He was a shabby fat man with bloodshot blue eyes, sad beaten eyes, and a big melancholy laugh, like a groan. He towered over them shouting to their father, "Well, for God's sake, Harry, it's been a coon's age. You ought to come out and look 'em over. You look just like yourself, Harry, how are you?"

The band struck up "Over the River" and Uncle Gabriel shouted louder. "Come on, let's get out of this. What are you doing up here with the pikers?"

"Can't," shouted Father. "Brought my little girls. Here they are."

Uncle Gabriel's bleared eyes beamed blindly upon them. "Fine looking set, Harry," he bellowed, "pretty as pictures, how old are they?"

"Ten and fourteen now," said Father; "awkward

ages. Nest of vipers," he boasted, "perfect batch of serpent's teeth. Can't do a thing with 'em." He fluffed up Miranda's hair, pretending to tousle it.

"Pretty as pictures," bawled Uncle Gabriel, "but rolled into one they don't come up to Amy, do they?"

"No, they don't," admitted their father at the top of his voice, "but they're only half-baked." *Over the river, over the river,* moaned the band, *my sweetheart's waiting for me.*

"I've got to get back now," yelled Uncle Gabriel. The little girls felt quite deaf and confused. "Got the God-damnedest jockey in the world, Harry, just my luck. Ought to tie him on. Fell off Fiddler yesterday, just plain fell off on his tail— Remember Amy's mare, Miss Lucy? Well, this is her namesake, Miss Lucy IV. None of 'em ever came up to the first one, though. Stay right where you are, I'll be back."

Maria spoke up boldly. "Uncle Gabriel, tell Miss Lucy we're betting on her." Uncle Gabriel bent down and it looked as if there were tears in his swollen eyes. "God bless your sweet heart," he bellowed, "I'll tell her." He plunged down through the crowd again, his fat back bowed slightly in his loose clothes, his thick neck rolling over his collar.

Miranda and Maria, disheartened by the odds, by their first sight of their romantic Uncle Gabriel, whose language was so coarse, sat listlessly without watching, their chances missed, their dollars gone, their hearts sore. They didn't even move until their father leaned over and hauled them up. "Watch your horse," he said, in a quick warning voice, "watch Miss Lucy come home."

They stood up, scrambled to their feet on the bench, every vein in them suddenly beating so violently they could hardly focus their eyes, and saw a thin little mahogany-colored streak flash by the judges' stand, only a neck ahead, but their Miss Lucy, oh, their darling, their lovely—oh, Miss Lucy, their Uncle Gabriel's Miss Lucy, had won, had won. They leaped up and down screaming and clapping their hands, their hats falling back on their shoulders, their hair flying wild. *Whoa, you heifer*, squalled the band with snorting brasses, and the crowd broke into a long roar like the falling of the walls of Jericho.

The little girls sat down, feeling quite dizzy, while their father tried to pull their hats straight, and taking out his handkerchief held it to Miranda's face, saying very gently, "Here, blow your nose," and he dried her eyes while he was about it. He stood up then and shook them out of their daze. He was smiling with deep laughing wrinkles around his eyes, and spoke to them as if they were grown young ladies he was squiring around.

"Let's go out and pay our respects to Miss Lucy," he said. "She's the star of the day."

The horses were coming in, looking as if their hides had been drenched and rubbed with soap, their ribs heaving, their nostrils flaring and closing. The jockeys sat bowed and relaxed, their faces calm, moving a little at the waist with the movement of their horses. Miranda noted this for future use; that was the way you came in from a race, easy and quiet, whether you had won or lost. Miss Lucy came last, and a little handful of winners applauded her and cheered the jockey. He smiled and lifted his whip, his eyes and shriveled brown face perfectly serene. Miss Lucy was bleeding at the nose, two thick red rivulets were stiffening her tender mouth and chin, the round velvet chin that Miranda thought the nicest kind of chin in the world. Her eyes were wild and her knees were trembling, and she snored when she drew her breath.

Miranda stood staring. That was winning, too. Her heart clinched tight; that was winning, for Miss Lucy. So instantly and completely did her heart reject that victory, she did not know when it happened, but she hated it, and was ashamed that she had screamed and shed tears for joy when Miss Lucy, with her bloodied nose and bursting heart had gone past the judges' stand a neck ahead. She felt empty and sick and held to her father's hand so hard that he shook her off a little impatiently and said, "What is the matter with you? Don't be so fidgety."

Uncle Gabriel was standing there waiting, and he was completely drunk. He watched the mare go in, then leaned against the fence with its white-washed posts and sobbed openly. "She's got the nosebleed, Harry," he said. "Had it since yesterday. We thought we had her all fixed up. But she did it, all right. She's got a heart like a lion. I'm going to breed her, Harry. Her heart's worth a million dollars, by itself, God bless her." Tears ran over his brick-colored face and into his straggling mustaches. "If anything happens to her now I'll blow my brains out. She's my last hope. She saved my life. I've had a run," he said, groaning into a large handkerchief and mopping his face all over, "I've had a run of luck that would break a brass billy goat. God, Harry, let's go somewhere and have a drink."

"I must get the children back to school first, Gabriel," said their father, taking each by a hand.

"No, no, don't go yet," said Uncle Gabriel desperately. "Wait here a minute, I want to see the vet and take a look at Miss Lucy, and I'll be right back. Don't go, Harry, for God's sake. I want to talk to you a few minutes."

Maria and Miranda, watching Uncle Gabriel's lumbering, unsteady back, were thinking that this was the first time they had ever seen a man that they knew to be drunk. They had seen pictures and read descriptions, and had heard descriptions, so they recognized the symptoms at once. Miranda felt it was an important moment in a great many ways.

"Uncle Gabriel's a drunkard, isn't he?" she asked her father, rather proudly.

"Hush, don't say such things," said Father, with a heavy frown, "or I'll never bring you here again." He looked worried and unhappy, and, above all, undecided. The little girls stood stiff with resentment against such obvious injustice. They loosed their hands from his and moved away coldly, standing together in silence. Their father did not notice, watching the place where Uncle Gabriel had disappeared. In a few minutes he came back, still wiping his face, as if there were cobwebs on it, carrying his big black hat. He waved at them from a short distance, calling out in a cheerful way, "She's going to be all right, Harry. It's stopped now. Lord, this will be good news for Miss Honey. Come on, Harry, let's all go home and tell Miss Honey. She deserves some good news."

Father said, "I'd better take the children back to school first, then we'll go."

"No, no," said Uncle Gabriel, fondly. "I want her to see the girls. She'll be tickled pink to see them, Harry. Bring 'em along."

"Is it another race horse we're going to see?" whispered Miranda in her sister's ear.

"Don't be silly," said Maria. "It's Uncle Gabriel's second wife."

"Let's find a cab, Harry," said Uncle Gabriel, "and take your little girls out to cheer up Miss Honey. Both of 'em rolled into one look a lot like Amy, I swear they do. I want Miss Honey to see them. She's always liked our family, Harry, though of course she's not what you'd call an expansive kind of woman."

Maria and Miranda sat facing the driver, and Uncle Gabriel squeezed himself in facing them beside their father. The air became at once bitter and sour with his breathing. He looked sad and poor. His necktie was on crooked and his shirt was rumpled. Father said, "You're going to see Uncle Gabriel's second wife, children," exactly as if they had not heard everything; and to Gabriel, "How *is* your wife nowadays? It must be twenty years since I saw her last."

"She's pretty gloomy, and that's a fact," said Uncle Gabriel. "She's been pretty gloomy for years now, and nothing seems to shake her out of it. She never did care for horses, Harry, if you remember; she hasn't been near the track three times since we were married. When I think how Amy wouldn't have missed a race for anything . . . She's very different from Amy, Harry, a very different kind of woman. As fine a woman as ever lived in her own way, but she hates change and moving around, and she just lives in the boy."

"Where is Gabe now?" asked Father.

"Finishing college," said Uncle Gabriel; "a smart boy, but awfully like his mother. Awfully like," he said, in a melancholy way. "She hates being away from him. Just wants to sit down in the same town and wait for him to get through with his education. Well, I'm sorry it can't be done if that's what she wants, but God Almighty— And this last run of luck has about got her down. I hope you'll be able to cheer her up a little, Harry, she needs it."

The little girls sat watching the streets grow duller and dingier and narrower, and at last the shabbier and shabbier white people gave way to dressed-up Negroes, and then to shabby Negroes, and after a long way the cab stopped before a desolate-looking little hotel in Elysian Fields. Their father helped Maria and Miranda out, told the cabman to wait, and they followed Uncle Gabriel through a dirty damp-smelling patio, down a long gas-lighted hall full of a terrible smell, Miranda couldn't decide what it was made of but it had a bitter taste even, and up a long staircase with a ragged carpet. Uncle

Gabriel pushed open a door without warning, saying, "Come in, here we are."

A tall pale-faced woman with faded straw-colored
hair and pink-rimmed eyelids rose suddenly from a
squeaking rocking chair. She wore a stiff blue-and-
white-striped shirtwaist and a stiff black skirt of
some hard shiny material. Her large knuckled hands
rose to her round, neat pompadour at sight of her
visitors.

"Honey," said Uncle Gabriel, with large false
heartiness, "you'll never guess who's come to see
you." He gave her a clumsy hug. Her face did not
change and her eyes rested steadily on the three
strangers. "Amy's brother Harry, Honey, you remember, don't you?"

"Of course," said Miss Honey, putting out her
hand straight as a paddle, "of course I remember
you, Harry." She did not smile.

"And Amy's two little nieces," went on Uncle
Gabriel, bringing them forward. They put out their
hands limply, and Miss Honey gave each one a slight
flip and dropped it. "And we've got good news for
you," went on Uncle Gabriel, trying to bolster up
the painful situation. "Miss Lucy stepped out and
showed 'em today, Honey. We're rich again, old girl,
cheer up."

Miss Honey turned her long, despairing face toward her visitors. "Sit down," she said with a heavy
sigh, seating herself and motioning toward various
rickety chairs. There was a big lumpy bed, with a
grayish-white counterpane on it, a marble-topped

151

washstand, grayish coarse lace curtains on strings
at the two small windows, a small closed fireplace
with a hole in it for a stovepipe, and two trunks,
standing at odds as if somebody were just moving
in, or just moving out. Everything was dingy and
soiled and neat and bare; not a pin out of place.

"We'll move to the St. Charles tomorrow," said
Uncle Gabriel, as much to Harry as to his wife. "Get
your best dresses together, Honey, the long dry spell
is over."

Miss Honey's nostrils pinched together and she
rocked slightly, with her arms folded. "I've lived in
the St. Charles before, and I've lived here before,"
she said, in a tight deliberate voice, "and this time
I'll just stay where I am, thank you. I prefer it to
moving back here in three months. I'm settled now,
I feel at home here," she told him, glancing at
Harry, her pale eyes kindling with blue fire, a stiff
white line around her mouth.

The little girls sat trying not to stare, miserably
ill at ease. Their grandmother had pronounced
Harry's children to be the most unteachable she had
ever seen in her long experience with the young; but
they had learned by indirection one thing well—nice
people did not carry on quarrels before outsiders.
Family quarrels were sacred, to be waged privately
in fierce hissing whispers, low choked mutters and
growls. If they did yell and stamp, it must be behind
closed doors and windows. Uncle Gabriel's second
wife was hopping mad and she looked ready to fly
out at Uncle Gabriel any second, with him sitting

there like a hound when someone shakes a whip at him.

"She loathes and despises everybody in this room," thought Miranda, coolly, "and she's afraid we won't know it. She needn't worry, we knew it when we came in." With all her heart she wanted to go, but her father, though his face was a study, made no move. He seemed to be trying to think of something pleasant to say. Maria, feeling guilty, though she couldn't think why, was calculating rapidly, "Why, she's only Uncle Gabriel's second wife, and Uncle Gabriel was only married before to Aunt Amy, why, she's no kin at all, and I'm glad of it." Sitting back easily, she let her hands fall open in her lap; they would be going in a few minutes, undoubtedly, and they need never come back.

Then Father said, "We mustn't be keeping you, we just dropped in for a few minutes. We wanted to see how you are."

Miss Honey said nothing, but she made a little gesture with her hands, from the wrist, as if to say, "Well, you see how I am, and now what next?"

"I must take these young ones back to school," said Father, and Uncle Gabriel said stupidly, "Look, Honey, don't you think they resemble Amy a little? Especially around the eyes, especially Maria, don't you think, Harry?"

Their father glanced at them in turn. "I really couldn't say," he decided, and the little girls saw he was more monstrously embarrassed than ever. He turned to Miss Honey. "I hadn't seen Gabriel for so many years," he said, "we thought of getting out for a talk about old times together. You know how it is."

"Yes, I know," said Miss Honey, rocking a little, and all that she knew gleamed forth in a pallid, unquenchable hatred and bitterness that seemed enough to bring her long body straight up out of the chair in a fury, "I know," and she sat staring at the floor. Her mouth shook and straightened. There was a terrible silence, which was broken when the little girls saw their father rise. They got up, too, and it was all they could do to keep from making a dash for the door.

"I must get the young ones back," said their father. "They've had enough excitement for one day. They each won a hundred dollars on Miss Lucy. It was a good race," he said, in complete wretchedness, as if he simply could not extricate himself from the situation. "Wasn't it, Gabriel?"

"It was a grand race," said Gabriel, brokenly, "a grand race."

Miss Honey stood up and moved a step toward the door. "Do you take them to the races, actually?" she asked, and her lids flickered toward them as if they were loathsome insects, Maria felt.

"If I feel they deserve a little treat, yes," said their father, in an easy tone but with wrinkled brow.

"I had rather, much rather," said Miss Honey clearly, "see my son dead at my feet than hanging around a race track."

The next few moments were rather a blank, but at last they were out of it, going down the stairs, across the patio, with Uncle Gabriel seeing them back into the cab. His face was sagging, the features had fallen as if the flesh had slipped from the bones, and his eyelids were puffed and blue. "Good-by, Harry," he said soberly. "How long you expect to be here?"

"Starting back tomorrow," said Harry. "Just dropped in on a little business and to see how the girls were getting along."

"Well," said Uncle Gabriel, "I may be dropping into your part of the country one of these days. Good-by, children," he said, taking their hands one after the other in his big warm paws. "They're nice children, Harry. I'm glad you won on Miss Lucy," he said to the little girls, tenderly. "Don't spend your money foolishly, now. Well, so long, Harry." As the cab jolted away he stood there fat and sagging, holding up his arm and wagging his hand at them.

"Goodness," said Maria, in her most grown-up manner, taking her hat off and hanging it over her knee, "I'm glad that's over."

"What I want to know is," said Miranda, "*is* Uncle Gabriel a real drunkard?"

"Oh, hush," said their father, sharply, "I've got the heartburn."

There was a respectful pause, as before a public monument. When their father had the heartburn it was time to lay low. The cab rumbled on, back to clean gay streets, with the lights coming on in the early February darkness, past shimmering shop windows, smooth pavements, on and on, past beautiful old houses set in deep gardens, on, on back to the dark walls with the heavy-topped trees hanging over them. Miranda sat thinking so hard she forgot and spoke out in her thoughtless way: "I've decided I'm not going to be a jockey, after all." She could as usual have bitten her tongue, but as usual it was too late.

Father cheered up and twinkled at her knowingly, as if that didn't surprise him in the least. "Well, well," said he, "so you aren't going to be a jockey! That's very sensible of you. I think she ought to be a lion-tamer, don't you, Maria? That's a nice, womanly profession."

Miranda, seeing Maria from the height of her fourteen years suddenly joining with their father to laugh at her, made an instant decision and laughed with them at herself. That was better. Everybody laughed and it was such a relief.

"Where's my hundred dollars?" asked Maria, anxiously.

"It's going in the bank," said their father, "and yours too," he told Miranda. "That is your nest-egg."

"Just so they don't buy my stockings with it," said Miranda, who had long resented the use of her Christmas money by their grandmother. "I've got enough stockings to last me a year."

"I'd like to buy a racehorse," said Maria, "but I know it's not enough." The limitations of wealth oppressed her. "*What* could you buy with a hundred dollars?" she asked fretfully.

"Nothing, nothing at all," said their father, "a

hundred dollars is just something you put in the bank."

Maria and Miranda lost interest. They had won a hundred dollars on a horse race once. It was already in the far past. They began to chatter about something else.

The lay sister opened the door on a long cord, from behind the grille; Maria and Miranda walked in silently to their familiar world of shining bare floors and insipid wholesome food and cold-water washing and regular prayers; their world of poverty, chastity and obedience, of early to bed and early to rise, of sharp little rules and tittle-tattle. Resignation was in their childish faces as they held them up to be kissed.

"Be good girls," said their father, in the strange serious, rather helpless way he always had when he told them good-by. "Write to your daddy, now, nice long letters," he said, holding their arms firmly for a moment before letting go for good. Then he disappeared, and the sister swung the door closed after him.

Maria and Miranda went upstairs to the dormitory to wash their faces and hands and slick down their hair again before supper.

Miranda was hungry. "We didn't have a thing to eat, after all," she grumbled. "Not even a chocolate nut bar. I think that's mean. We didn't even get a quarter to spend," she said.

"Not a living bite," said Maria. "Not a nickel." She poured out cold water into the bowl and rolled up her sleeves.

Another girl about her own age came in and went to a washbowl near another bed. "Where have you been?" she asked. "Did you have a good time?"

"We went to the races, with our father," said Maria, soaping her hands.

"Our uncle's horse won," said Miranda.

"My goodness," said the other girl, vaguely, "that must have been grand."

Maria looked at Miranda, who was rolling up her own sleeves. She tried to feel martyred, but it wouldn't go. "Immured for another week," she said, her eyes sparkling over the edge of her towel.

Part III: 1912

Miranda followed the porter down the stuffy aisle of the sleeping-car, where the berths were nearly all made down and the dusty green curtains buttoned, to a seat at the further end. "Now yo' berth's ready any time, Miss," said the porter.

"But I want to sit up a while," said Miranda. A very thin old lady raised choleric black eyes and fixed upon her a regard of unmixed disapproval. She had two immense front teeth and a receding chin, but she did not lack character. She had piled her luggage around her like a barricade, and she glared at the porter when he picked some of it up to make room for his new passenger. Miranda sat, saying mechanically, "May I?"

"You may, indeed," said the old lady, for she seemed old in spite of a certain brisk, rustling energy. Her taffeta petticoats creaked like hinges every time she stirred. With ferocious sarcasm, after a half-second's pause, she added, "You may be so good as to get off my hat!"

Miranda rose instantly in horror, and handed to the old lady a wilted contrivance of black horsehair braid and shattered white poppies. "I'm dreadfully sorry," she stammered, for she had been brought up to treat ferocious old ladies respectfully, and this one seemed capable of spanking her, then and there. "I didn't dream it was your hat."

"And whose hat did you dream it might be?" inquired the old lady, baring her teeth and twirling the hat on a forefinger to restore it.

"I didn't think it was a hat at all," said Miranda with a touch of hysteria.

"Oh, you didn't think it was a hat? Where on earth are your eyes, child?" and she proved the nature and function of the object by placing it on her head at a somewhat tipsy angle, though still it did not much resemble a hat. "Now can you see what it is?"

"Yes, oh, yes," said Miranda, with a meekness she hoped was disarming. She ventured to sit again after a careful inspection of the narrow space she was to occupy.

"Well, well," said the old lady, "let's have the porter remove some of these encumbrances," and she stabbed the bell with a lean sharp forefinger. There followed a flurry of rearrangements, during which they both stood in the aisle, the old lady giving a series of impossible directions to the Negro which he bore philosophically while he disposed of the luggage exactly as he had meant to do. Seated again, the old lady asked in a kindly, authoritative tone, "And what might your name be, child?"

At Miranda's answer, she blinked somewhat, unfolded her spectacles, straddled them across her high nose competently, and took a good long look at the face beside her.

"If I'd had my spectacles on," she said, in an astonishingly changed voice, "I might have known. I'm Cousin Eva Parrington," she said, "Cousin Molly Parrington's daughter, remember? I knew you when you were a little girl. You were a lively little girl," she added as if to console her, "and very opinionated. The last thing I heard about you, you were planning to be a tight-rope walker. You were going to play the violin and walk the tight rope at the same time."

"I must have seen it at the vaudeville show," said Miranda. "I couldn't have invented it. Now I'd like to be an air pilot!"

"I used to go to dances with your father," said Cousin Eva, busy with her own thoughts, "and to big holiday parties at your grandmother's house, long before you were born. Oh, indeed, yes, a long time before."

Miranda remembered several things at once. Aunt Amy had threatened to be an old maid like Eva. Oh, Eva, the trouble with her is she has no chin. Eva has given up, and is teaching Latin in a Female Seminary. Eva's gone out for votes for women, God help her. The nice thing about an ugly daughter is, she's not apt to make me a grandmother. . . . "They didn't do you much good, those parties, dear Cousin Eva," thought Miranda.

"They didn't do me much good, those parties," said Cousin Eva aloud as if she were a mind-reader, and Miranda's head swam for a moment with fear that she had herself spoken aloud. "Or at least, they didn't serve their purpose, for I never got married; but I enjoyed them, just the same. I had a good time at those parties, even if I wasn't a belle. And so you are Harry's child, and here I was quarreling with you. You do remember me, don't you?"

"Yes," said Miranda, and thinking that even if Cousin Eva had been really an old maid ten years before, still she couldn't be much past fifty now, and she looked so withered and tired, so famished and sunken in the cheeks, so *old*, somehow. Across the abyss separating Cousin Eva from her own youth, Miranda looked with painful premonition. "Oh, must I ever be like that?" She said aloud, "Yes, you used to read Latin to me, and tell me not to bother about the sense, to get the sound in my mind, and it would come easier later."

"Ah, so I did," said Cousin Eva, delighted. "So I did. You don't happen to remember that I once had a beautiful sapphire velvet dress with a train on it?"

"No, I don't remember that dress," said Miranda.

"It was an old dress of my mother's made over and cut down to fit," said Eva, "and it wasn't in the least becoming to me, but it was the only really good dress I ever had, and I remember it as if it were yesterday. Blue was never my color." She sighed with a humorous bitterness. The humor seemed momentary, but the bitterness was a constant state of mind.

Miranda, trying to offer the sympathy of fellow suffering, said, "I know. I've had Maria's dresses made over for me, and they were never right. It was dreadful."

"Well," said Cousin Eva, in the tone of one who did not wish to share her unique disappointments. "How is your father? I always liked him. He was one of the finest-looking young men I ever saw. Vain, too, like all his family. He wouldn't ride any but the best horses he could buy, and I used to say he made them prance and then watched his own shadow. I used to tell this on him at dinner parties, and he hated me for it. I feel pretty certain he hated me." An overtone of complacency in Cousin Eva's voice explained better than words that she had her own method of commanding attention and arousing emotion. "How *is* your father, I asked you, my dear?"

"I haven't seen him for nearly a year," answered Miranda, quickly, before Cousin Eva could get ahead again. "I'm going home now to Uncle Gabriel's funeral; you know, Uncle Gabriel died in Lexington and they have brought him back to be buried beside Aunt Amy."

"So that's how we meet," said Cousin Eva. "Yes, Gabriel drank himself to death at last. I'm going to the funeral, too. I haven't been home since I went to Mother's funeral, it must be, let's see, yes, it will be nine years next July. I'm going to Gabriel's funeral, though. I wouldn't miss that. Poor fellow, what a life he had. Pretty soon, they'll all be gone."

Miranda said, "We're left, Cousin Eva," meaning those of her own generation, the young, and Cousin Eva said, "Pshaw, you'll live forever, and you won't bother to come to our funerals." She didn't seem to think this was a misfortune, but flung the remark from her like a woman accustomed to saying what she thought.

Miranda sat thinking, "Still, I suppose it would be pleasant if I could say something to make her believe that she and all of them would be lamented, but—but—" With a smile which she hoped would be her denial of Cousin Eva's cynicism about the younger generation, she said, "You were right about the Latin, Cousin Eva, your reading did help when I began with it. I still study," she said. "Latin, too."

"And why shouldn't you?" asked Cousin Eva, sharply, adding at once mildly, "I'm glad you are going to use your mind a little, child. Don't let yourself rust away. Your mind outwears all sorts of things you may set your heart upon; you can enjoy it when all other things are taken away." Miranda was chilled by her melancholy. Cousin Eva went on: "In our part of the country, in my time, we were so provincial—a woman didn't dare to think or act for herself. The whole world was a little that way," she said, "but we were the worst, I believe. I suppose you must know how I fought for votes for women when it almost made a pariah of me—I was turned out of my chair at the Seminary, but I'm glad I did it and I would do it again. You young things don't realize. You'll live in a better world because we worked for it."

Miranda knew something of Cousin Eva's career. She said sincerely, "I think it was brave of you, and I'm glad you did it, too. I loved your courage."

"It wasn't just showing off, mind you," said

Cousin Eva, rejecting praise, fretfully. "Any fool can be brave. We were working for something we knew was right, and it turned out that we needed a lot of courage for it. That was all. I didn't expect to go to jail, but I went three times, and I'd go three times three more if it were necessary. We aren't voting yet," she said, "but we will be."

Miranda did not venture any answer, but she felt convinced that indeed women would be voting soon if nothing fatal happened to Cousin Eva. There was something in her manner which said such things could be left safely to her. Miranda was dimly fired for the cause herself; it seemed heroic and worth suffering for, but discouraging, too, to those who came after: Cousin Eva so plainly had swept the field clear of opportunity.

They were silent for a few minutes, while Cousin Eva rummaged in her handbag, bringing up odds and ends: peppermint drops, eye drops, a packet of needles, three handkerchiefs, a little bottle of violet perfume, a book of addresses, two buttons, one black, one white, and, finally, a packet of headache powders.

"Bring me a glass of water, will you, my dear?" she asked Miranda. She poured the headache powder on her tongue, swallowed the water, and put two peppermints in her mouth.

"So now they're going to bury Gabriel near Amy," she said after a while, as if her eased headache had started her on a new train of thought. "Miss Honey would like that, poor dear, if she could know. After listening to stories about Amy for twenty-five years, she must lie alone in her grave in Lexington while Gabriel sneaks off to Texas to make his bed with Amy again. It was a kind of life-long infidelity, Miranda, and now an eternal infidelity on top of that. He ought to be ashamed of himself."

"It was Aunt Amy he loved," said Miranda, wondering what Miss Honey could have been like before her long troubles with Uncle Gabriel. "First, anyway."

"Oh, that Amy," said Cousin Eva, her eyes glittering. "Your Aunt Amy was a devil and a mischiefmaker, but I loved her dearly. I used to stand up for Amy when her reputation wasn't worth that." Her fingers snapped like castanets. "She used to say to me, in that gay soft way she had, 'Now, Eva, don't go talking votes for women when the lads ask you to dance. Don't recite Latin poems to 'em,' she would say, 'they got sick of that in school. Dance and say nothing, Eva,' she would say, her eyes perfectly devilish, 'and hold your chin up, Eva.' My chin was my weak point, you see. 'You'll never catch a husband if you don't look out,' she would say. Then she would laugh and fly away, and where did she fly to?" demanded Cousin Eva, her sharp eyes pinning Miranda down to the bitter facts of the case, "To scandal and to death, nowhere else."

"She was joking, Cousin Eva," said Miranda, innocently, "and everybody loved her."

"Not everybody, by a long shot," said Cousin Eva in triumph. "She had enemies. If she knew, she pretended she didn't. If she cared, she never said. You couldn't make her quarrel. She was sweet as a honeycomb to everybody. *Everybody*," she added, "that was the trouble. She went through life like a spoiled darling, doing as she pleased and letting other people suffer for it, and pick up the pieces after her. I never believed for one moment," said Cousin Eva, putting her mouth close to Miranda's ear and breathing peppermint hotly into it, "that Amy was an impure woman. Never! But let me tell you, there were plenty who did believe it. There were plenty to pity poor Gabriel for being so completely blinded by her. A great many persons were not surprised when they heard that Gabriel was perfectly miserable all the time, on their honeymoon, in New Orleans. Jealousy. And why not? But I used to say to such persons that, no matter what the appearances were, I had faith in Amy's virtue. Wild, I said, indiscreet, I said, heartless, I said, but *virtuous*, I feel certain. But you could hardly blame anyone for being mystified. The way she rose up suddenly from death's door to marry Gabriel Breaux, after refusing him and treating him like a dog for years, looked odd, to say the least. To say the very least," she added, after a moment, "odd is a mild word for it. And there was something very mysterious about her death, only six weeks after marriage."

Miranda roused herself. She felt she knew this part of the story and could set Cousin Eva right about one thing. "She died of a hemorrhage from the lungs," said Miranda. "She had been ill for five years, don't you remember?"

Cousin Eva was ready for that. "Ha, that was the story, indeed. The official account, you might say.

Oh, yes, I heard that often enough. But did you ever hear about that fellow Raymond somebody-or-other from Calcasieu Parish, almost a stranger, who persuaded Amy to elope with him from a dance one night, and she just ran out into the darkness without even stopping for her cloak, and your poor dear nice father Harry—you weren't even thought of then—had to run him down to earth and shoot him?"

Miranda leaned back from the advancing flood of speech. "Cousin Eva, my father shot *at* him, don't you remember? He didn't hit him. . . ."

"Well, that's a pity."

". . . and they had only gone out for a breath of air between dances. It was Uncle Gabriel's jealousy. And my father shot at the man because he thought that was better than letting Uncle Gabriel fight a duel about Aunt Amy. There was *nothing* in the whole affair except Uncle Gabriel's jealousy."

"You poor baby," said Cousin Eva, and pity gave a light like daggers to her eyes, "you dear innocent, you—do you believe that? How old are you, anyway?"

"Just past eighteen," said Miranda.

"If you don't understand what I tell you," said Cousin Eva portentously, "you will later. Knowledge can't hurt you. You mustn't live in a romantic haze about life. You'll understand when you're married, at any rate."

"I'm married now, Cousin Eva," said Miranda, feeling for almost the first time that it might be an advantage, "nearly a year. I eloped from school."

It seemed very unreal even as she said it, and seemed to have nothing at all to do with the future; still, it was important, it must be declared, it was a situation in life which people seemed to be most exacting about, and the only feeling she could rouse in herself about it was an immense weariness as if it were an illness that she might one day hope to recover from.

"Shameful, shameful," cried Cousin Eva, genuinely repelled. "If you had been my child I should have brought you home and spanked you."

Miranda laughed out. Cousin Eva seemed to believe things could be arranged like that. She was so solemn and fierce, so comic and baffled.

"And you must know I should have just gone straight out again, through the nearest window," she taunted her. "If I went the first time, why not the second?"

"Yes, I suppose so," said Cousin Eva. "I hope you married rich."

"Not so very," said Miranda. "Enough." As if anyone could have stopped to think of such a thing!

Cousin Eva adjusted her spectacles and sized up Miranda's dress, her luggage, examined her engagement ring and wedding ring, with her nostrils fairly quivering as if she might smell out wealth on her.

"Well, that's better than nothing," said Cousin Eva. "I thank God every day of my life that I have a small income. It's a Rock of Ages. What would have become of me if I hadn't a cent of my own? Well, you'll be able now to do something for your family."

Miranda remembered what she had always heard

about the Parringtons. They were money-hungry, they loved money and nothing else, and when they had got some they kept it. Blood was thinner than water between the Parringtons where money was concerned.

"We're pretty poor," said Miranda, stubbornly allying herself with her father's family instead of her husband's, "but a rich marriage is no way out," she said, with the snobbishness of poverty. She was thinking, "You don't know my branch of the family, dear Cousin Eva, if you think it is."

"Your branch of the family," said Cousin Eva, with that terrifying habit she had of lifting phrases out of one's mind, "has no more practical sense than so many children. Everything for love," she said, with a face of positive nausea, "that was it. Gabriel would have been rich if his grandfather had not disinherited him, but would Amy be sensible and marry him and make him settle down so the old man would have been pleased with him? No. And what could Gabriel do without money? I wish you could have seen the life he led Miss Honey, one day buying her Paris gowns and the next day pawning her earrings. It just depended on how the horses ran, and they ran worse and worse, and Gabriel drank more and more."

Miranda did not say, "I saw a little of it." She was trying to imagine Miss Honey in a Paris gown. She said, "But Uncle Gabriel was so mad about Aunt Amy, there was no question of her not marrying him at last, money or no money."

Cousin Eva strained her lips tightly over her

teeth, let them fly again and leaned over, gripping Miranda's arm. "What I ask myself, what I ask myself over and over again," she whispered, "is, what connection did this man Raymond from Calcasieu have with Amy's sudden marriage to Gabriel, and *what* did Amy do to make away with herself so soon afterward? For mark my words, child, Amy wasn't so ill as all that. She'd been flying around for years after the doctors said her lungs were weak. Amy did away with herself to escape some disgrace, some exposure that she faced."

The beady black eyes glinted; Cousin Eva's face was quite frightening, so near and so intent. Miranda wanted to say, "Stop. Let her rest. What harm did she ever do you?" but she was timid and unnerved, and deep in her was a horrified fascination with the terrors and the darkness Cousin Eva had conjured up. What was the end of this story?

"She was a bad, wild girl, but I was fond of her to the last," said Cousin Eva. "She got into trouble somehow, and she couldn't get out again, and I have every reason to believe she killed herself with the drug they gave her to keep her quiet after a hemorrhage. If she didn't, what happened, what happened?"

"I don't know," said Miranda. "How should I know? She was very beautiful," she said, as if this explained everything. "Everybody said she was very beautiful."

"Not everybody," said Cousin Eva, firmly, shaking her head. "I for one never thought so. They made entirely too much fuss over her. She was good-looking enough, but why did they think she was beautiful? I cannot understand it. She was too thin when she was young, and later I always thought she was too fat, and again in her last year she was altogether too thin. She always got herself up to be looked at, and so people looked, of course. She rode too hard, and she danced too freely, and she talked too much, and you'd have to be blind, deaf and dumb not to notice her. I don't mean she was loud or vulgar, she wasn't, but she was *too free*," said Cousin Eva. She stopped for breath and put a peppermint in her mouth. Miranda could see Cousin Eva on the platform, making her speeches, stopping to take a peppermint. But why did she hate Aunt Amy so, when Aunt Amy was dead and she alive? Wasn't being alive enough?

"And her illness wasn't romantic either," said Cousin Eva, "though to hear them tell it she faded like a lily. Well, she coughed blood, if that's romantic. If they had made her take proper care of herself, if she had been nursed sensibly, she might have been alive today. But no, nothing of the kind. She lay wrapped in beautiful shawls on a sofa with flowers around her, eating as she liked or not eating, getting up after a hemorrhage and going out to ride or dance, sleeping with the windows closed; with crowds coming in and out laughing and talking at all hours, and Amy sitting up so her hair wouldn't get out of curl. And why wouldn't that sort of thing kill a well person in time? I have almost died twice in my life," said Cousin Eva, "and both times I was sent to a hospital where I belonged and left there until I came out. And I came out," she said, her voice deepening to a bugle note, "and I went to work again."

"Beauty goes, character stays," said the small voice of axiomatic morality in Miranda's ear. It was a dreary prospect; why was a strong character so deforming? Miranda felt she truly wanted to be strong, but how could she face it, seeing what it did to one?

"She had a lovely complexion," said Cousin Eva, "perfectly transparent with a flush on each cheekbone. But it was tuberculosis, and is disease beautiful? And she brought it on herself by drinking lemon and salt to stop her periods when she wanted to gc to dances. There was a superstition among young girls about that. They fancied that young men could tell what ailed them by touching their hands, or even by looking at them. As if it mattered? But they were terribly self-conscious and they had immense respect for man's worldly wisdom in those days. My own notion is that a man couldn't—but anyway, the whole thing was stupid."

"I should have thought they'd have stayed at home if they couldn't manage better than that," said Miranda, feeling very knowledgeable and modern.

"They didn't dare. Those parties and dances were their market, a girl couldn't afford to miss out, there were always rivals waiting to cut the ground from under her. The rivalry—" said Cousin Eva, and her head lifted, she arched like a cavalry horse getting a whiff of the battlefield—"you can't imagine what the rivalry was like. The way those girls treated each other—nothing was too mean, nothing too false—"

Cousin Eva wrung her hands. "It was just sex," she said in despair; "their minds dwelt on nothing else. They didn't call it that, it was all smothered under pretty names, but that's all it was, sex." She looked out of the window into the darkness, her sunken cheek near Miranda flushed deeply. She turned back. "I took to the soap box and the platform when I was called upon," she said proudly, "and I went to jail when it was necessary, and my condition didn't make any difference. I was booed and jeered and shoved around just as if I had been in perfect health. But it was part of our philosophy not to let our physical handicaps make any difference to our work. You know what I mean," she said, as if until now it was all mystery. "Well, Amy carried herself with more spirit than the others, and she didn't seem to be making any sort of fight, but she was simply sex-ridden, like the rest. She behaved as if she hadn't a rival on earth, and she pretended not to know what marriage was about, but I know better. None of them had, and they didn't want to have, anything else to think about, and they didn't really know anything about that, so they simply festered inside—they festered—"

Miranda found herself deliberately watching a long procession of living corpses, festering women stepping gaily toward the charnel house, their corruption concealed under laces and flowers, their dead faces lifted smiling, and thought quite coldly, "Of course it was not like that. This is no more true than what I was told before, it's every bit as romantic," and she realized that she was tired of her intense Cousin Eva, she wanted to go to sleep, she wanted to be at home, she wished it were tomorrow and she could see her father and her sister, who were so alive and solid; who would mention her freckles and ask her if she wanted something to eat.

"My mother was not like that," she said, childishly. "My mother was a perfectly natural woman who liked to cook. I have seen some of her sewing," she said. "I have read her diary."

"Your mother was a saint," said Cousin Eva, automatically.

Miranda sat silent, outraged. "My mother was nothing of the sort," she wanted to fling in Cousin Eva's big front teeth. But Cousin Eva had been gathering bitterness until more speech came of it.

" 'Hold your chin up, Eva,' Amy used to tell me," she began, doubling up both her fists and shaking them a little. "All my life the whole family bedeviled me about my chin. My entire girlhood was spoiled by it. Can you imagine," she asked, with a ferocity that seemed much too deep for this one cause, "people who call themselves civilized spoiling life for a young girl because she had one unlucky feature? Of course, you understand perfectly it was all in the very best humor, everybody was very amusing about it, no harm meant—oh, no, no harm at all. That is the hellish thing about it. It is that I can't forgive," she cried out, and she twisted her hands together as if they were rags. "Ah, the family," she said, releasing her breath and sitting back quietly, "the whole hideous institution should be wiped from the face of the earth. It is the root of all human wrongs," she ended, and relaxed, and her face became calm. She was trembling. Miranda reached out and took Cousin Eva's hand and held it. The hand fluttered and lay still, and Cousin Eva said, "You've not the faintest idea what some of us went through, but I wanted you to hear the other side of the story. And I'm keeping you up when you need your beauty sleep," she said grimly, stirring herself with an immense rustle of petticoats.

Miranda pulled herself together, feeling limp, and stood up. Cousin Eva put out her hand again, and drew Miranda down to her. "Good night, you dear child," she said, "to think you're grown up." Miranda hesitated, then quite suddenly kissed her Cousin Eva on the cheek. The black eyes shown brightly through water for an instant, and Cousin Eva said with a warm note in her sharp clear orator's voice, "Tomorrow we'll be at home again. I'm looking forward to it, aren't you? Good night."

Miranda fell asleep while she was getting off her clothes. Instantly it was morning again. She was still trying to close her suitcase when the train pulled into the small station, and there on the platform she saw her father, looking tired and anxious, his hat pulled over his eyes. She rapped on the window to catch his attention, then ran out and threw herself upon him. He said, "Well, here's my big girl," as if she were still seven, but his hands on her arms held her off, the tone was forced. There was no welcome for her, and there had not been since she had run away. She could not persuade herself to remem-

ber how it would be; between one home-coming and
the next her mind refused to accept its own knowledge. Her father looked over her head and said,
without surprise, "Why, hello, Eva, I'm glad somebody sent you a telegram." Miranda, rebuffed again,
let her arms fall away again, with the same painful
dull jerk of the heart.

"No one in my family," said Eva, her face framed
in the thin black veil she reserved, evidently, for
family funerals, "ever sent me a telegram in my life.
I had the news from young Keziah who had it from
young Gabriel. I suppose Gabe is here?"

"Everybody seems to be here," said Father. "The
house is getting full."

"I'll go to the hotel if you like," said Cousin Eva.

"Damnation, no," said Father. "I didn't mean
that. You'll come with us where you belong."

Skid, the handy man, grabbed the suitcases and
started down the rocky village street. "We've got
the car," said Father. He took Miranda by the hand,
then dropped it again, and reached for Cousin Eva's
elbow.

"I'm perfectly able, thank you," said Cousin Eva,
shying away.

"If you're so independent now," said Father,
"God help us when you get that vote."

Cousin Eva pushed back her veil. She was smiling
merrily. She liked Harry, she always had liked him,
he could tease as much as he liked. She slipped her
arm through his. "So it's all over with poor Gabriel,
isn't it?"

"Oh, yes," said Father, "it's all over, all right.

They're pegging out pretty regularly now. It will be our turn next, Eva?"

"I don't know, and I don't care," said Eva, recklessly. "It's good to be back now and then, Harry, even if it is only for funerals. I feel sinfully cheerful."

"Oh, Gabriel wouldn't mind, he'd like seeing you cheerful. Gabriel was the cheerfulest cuss I ever saw, when we were young. Life for Gabriel," said Father, "was just one perpetual picnic."

"Poor fellow," said Cousin Eva.

"Poor old Gabriel," said Father, heavily.

Miranda walked along beside her father, feeling homeless, but not sorry for it. He had not forgiven her, she knew that. When would he? She could not guess, but she felt it would come of itself, without words and without acknowledgment on either side, for by the time it arrived neither of them would need to remember what had caused their division, nor why it had seemed so important. Surely old people cannot hold their grudges forever because the young want to live, too, she thought, in her arrogance, her pride. I will make my own mistakes, not yours; I cannot depend upon you beyond a certain point, why depend at all? There was something more beyond, but this was a first step to take, and she took it, walking in silence beside her elders who were no longer Cousin Eva and Father, since they had forgotten her presence, but had become Eva and Harry, who knew each other well, who were comfortable with each other, being contemporaries on equal terms, who occupied by right their place in this world, at the time of life to which they had arrived by paths familiar to them both. They need not play their roles of daughter, of son, to aged persons who did not understand them; nor of father and elderly female cousin to young persons whom they did not understand. They were precisely themselves; their eyes cleared, their voices relaxed into perfect naturalness, they need not weigh their words or calculate the effect of their manner. "It is I who have no place," thought Miranda. "Where are my own people and my own time?" She resented, slowly and deeply and in profound silence, the presence of these aliens who lectured and admonished her, who loved her with bitterness and denied her the right to look at the world with her own eyes, who demanded that she accept their version of life and yet could not tell her the truth, not in the smallest thing. "I hate them both," her most inner and secret mind said plainly, "*I will be free of them, I shall not even remember them.*"

She sat in the front seat with Skid, the Negro boy. "Come back with us, Miranda," said Cousin Eva, with the sharp little note of elderly command, "there is plenty of room."

"No, thank you," said Miranda, in a firm cold voice. "I'm quite comfortable. Don't disturb yourself."

Neither of them noticed her voice or her manner. They sat back and went on talking steadily in their friendly family voices, talking about their dead, their living, their affairs, their prospects, their common memories, interrupting each other, catching each other up on small points of dispute, laughing with a gaiety and freshness Miranda had not known they were capable of, going over old stories and finding new points of interest in them.

Miranda could not hear the stories above the noisy motor, but she felt she knew them well, or stories like them. She knew too many stories like them, she wanted something new of her own. The language was familiar to them, but not to her, not any more. The house, her father had said, was full. It would be full of cousins, many of them strangers. Would there be any young cousins there, to whom she could talk about things they both knew? She felt a vague distaste for seeing cousins. There were too many of them and her blood rebelled against the ties of blood. She was sick to death of cousins. She did not want any more ties with this house, she was going to leave it, and she was not going back to her husband's family either. She would have no more bonds that smothered her in love and hatred. She knew now why she had run away to marriage, and she knew that she was going to run away from marriage, and she was not going to stay in any place, with anyone, that threatened to forbid her making her own discoveries, that said "No" to her. She hoped no one had taken her old room, she would like to sleep there once more, she would say good-by there where she had loved sleeping once, sleeping and waking and waiting to be grown, to begin to live. Oh, what is life, she asked herself in desperate seriousness, in those childish unanswerable words, and what shall I do with it? It is something of my own, she thought in a fury of jealous possessiveness, what shall I make of it? She did not know that she asked herself this because all her earliest training had argued that life was a substance, a material to be used, it took shape and direction and meaning only as the possessor guided and worked it; living was a progress of continuous and varied acts of the will directed toward a definite end. She had been assured that there were good and evil ends, one must make a choice. But what was good, and what was evil? I hate love, she thought, as if this were the answer, I hate loving and being loved, I hate it. And her disturbed and seething mind received a shock of comfort from this sudden collapse of an old painful structure of distorted images and misconceptions. "You don't know anything about it," said Miranda to herself, with extraordinary clearness as if she were an elder admonishing some younger misguided creature. "You have to find out about it." But nothing in her prompted her to decide, "I will now do this, I will be that, I will go yonder, I will take a certain road to a certain end." There are questions to be asked first, she thought, but who will answer them? No one, or there will be too many answers, none of them right. What is the truth, she asked herself as intently as if the question had never been asked, the truth, even about the smallest, the least important of all the things I must find out? and where shall I begin to look for it? Her mind closed stubbornly against remembering, not the past but the legend of the past, other people's memory of the past, at which she had spent her life peering in wonder like a child at a magic-lantern show. Ah, but there is my own life to come yet, she thought, my own life now and beyond. I don't want any promises, I won't have false hopes, I won't be romantic about myself. I can't live in their world any longer, she told herself, listening to the voices back of her. Let them tell their stories to each other. Let them go on explaining how things happened. I don't care. At least I can know the truth about what happens to me, she assured herself silently, making a promise to herself, in her hopefulness, her ignorance.